THE SECRETS NEXT DOOR

SALLY ROYER-DERR

To request permissions, contact the publisher at rights@stormpublishing.co

Ebook ISBN: 978-1-80508-158-6
Paperback ISBN: 978-1-80508-402-0

Cover design: Jules Macadam
Cover images: Shutterstock

Published by Storm Publishing.
For further information, visit:
www.stormpublishing.co

For Mike, my favorite person in the world

PROLOGUE

Barely any moonlight is visible on the chilly, late autumn night. The cold reaches its icy fingers around me as I stumble to the water's edge. Ripples dance through the once calm water, a frosty gale breaking the otherwise still surroundings. A few minutes pass and the melody concludes. Fear constricts my throat as I am forced along. Nobody hears my screams in this darkness.

Dry scattered leaves litter the ground, some smashed into it: the result of heavy footsteps in the soft earth.

Hands press into my arms, strong and unyielding, pushing me into the dark, cold water. My heart races, thundering inside my chest. I don't want to die here. A scream escapes me, and another, as I struggle with my assailant. The long, bright red ribbon in my hair falls, landing on the surface of the water. I'm pushed into its inky darkness, my line of sight on the ribbon absorbing the water around it.

Hands shove me under the water. I fight, clawing at my attacker, but I'm no match for their strength. My head pops above the water for a moment. I gasp, air filling my lungs for the last time, then I'm pushed down again, and again, by heavy hands, water replacing the air. Help me! I scream again, but, again, nobody hears my cry. I weaken; my head hangs down.

Moonlight trickles downward, illuminating the dark water for a moment. The last image I see is the red and white pleated skirt of the cheerleader costume I'm wearing. My mind blackens and my body sinks into its watery grave.

ONE

TALIA

I place the last group of brightly colored metallic blue and green balloons at the edge of the already decorated table, only a few inches away from the lavish dinosaur themed birthday cake, one that gave me so much joy decorating. I adjust the streamers around the edge of the table and move the cupcakes, with miniature dinosaur eggs on top, in a semi-circle around the cake, the main attraction, of course. Only the best for my nephew's sixth birthday party.

"Talia, we're going to need more chairs out here. Should I send Grant to get more from our house?"

I turn, facing my twin sister, Tabitha. Her hands press into each side of her hips on the white Lilly Pulitzer dress that hangs on her toned frame, and an exasperated expression covers her face. Pretty much how she always looks at me.

"Probably," I say. "I thought we would have enough. How many people did you invite?"

"Well, I did invite a few more than the original guest list. I guess I was thinking we were having the party in my backyard, rather than yours, which is obviously much smaller. I hope we aren't too cramped." Tabitha purses her lips together.

I roll my eyes. The lack of lawn chairs is such a dire emergency. Tabitha always exaggerates everything. And, of course, nothing of mine could ever compare to what she has. Even though I graciously agreed to host her son, Cole's, birthday party, for some reason she acts as if she is doing me a favor. Never mind that her backyard has been under construction for several weeks. Tabitha and her husband, Grant, are putting in their backyard oasis—her words. In-ground pool, hot tub, tiki bar, new patio, firepit area, the works. Only the best for Tabitha. She could have easily rented a room at the country club for the party. But I don't mind. I am happy to have Cole's party at my house. I would, however, at least like a thank you.

"Obviously," I say, biting back the words I really want to say.

"And where is the wine station?" Tabitha asks, running a hand through her thick, honey-blonde hair. Thicker than mine. Shinier, too. "The PTA ladies need their wine, especially Nancy."

"The wine is in the kitchen. I thought that made more sense since it is a child's party," I reply.

"Yes, I guess that makes sense." She nods. "I'm going to grab a glass before I get Grant to dig more chairs out of our garage."

I nod, and she bounces off to find Grant, to fix the chair issue. I watch her stride away and for the millionth time wonder how she and I are sisters, twins even.

I love my sister. I truly do; but thirty-two years of being second best has done a number on my self-esteem. In my younger years, I aimlessly followed behind her, but lately, my irritation with her has grown. I didn't always want to be in her shadow. Part of me wants to be completely independent of her, but the other part has no idea how that would work. She is part of me.

Due to my choices, now I live next door to her and run a bakery with her, we're together all the time, like it's always been. Pangs of independence exist in me, the desire to be my own person, but there's no follow-through.

I shouldn't complain. Life is pretty good. Comfortable house in the suburbs, only a short train ride into the city. Tabitha and I often go into Manhattan for lunch and shopping, sometimes a show in the theater district. Now, our business is thriving. Our reputation high throughout Little Beak, NY and beyond for our specialty cakes and cupcakes. Tabitha is the baker, and I am the decorator. Little Beak Sweets started small in Tabitha's home kitchen. Now we have a store on Main Street in the upscale town. I love decorating cakes. It's an art form to me. My creations can be cute and whimsical or elegant and chic. Even sassy and funny. I always do my best to create whatever theme the customer sees in their mind for their occasion.

"Hey, Talia, where do you want me to set this up?" A tall, handsome man with stylish, neatly clipped dark hair emerges from the French doors on the patio. Zach. My husband. He holds a dinosaur pinata in his right hand.

"Oh, hang it on the tree over here." I point.

"Whatever you say, beautiful," Zach says, winking at me.

"Always a charmer," I tease back. "Just not too high."

"So, six-year-old height."

"Right." I laugh.

He smiles at me and nods, going about his task. I turn back to the cake table and eye it one more time to make sure everything is in order. Zach. Kind, loving Zach is the one thing I have but Tabitha does not. Sure, she has Grant, a nice guy, if a bit consumed with himself. But Zach is thoughtful, attentive, sometimes a bit overemotional, but that's better than distant, in my opinion.

Zach grew up with us in our little town in the Finger Lakes area. We'd been neighbors and friends since childhood, nestled in the beautiful town of Watkins Glen. I always harbored a crush on him, but he'd had an unrequited crush on Tabitha, at least until after college, when we started dating. We fell hard for each other. Love, marriage, a life together. Hopefully, one day, a baby. It's something we dream about happening in our lives. But every month comes the hope and then the disappointment. Tabitha frequently asks when we are going to have a baby, even though she knows that we are trying but it's not happening. If I mention to her how I don't want constant reminders of our struggle, her response would be I'm being oversensitive. I'm the sensitive one in the family. Like that's a bad thing. But Zach is always there for me. He is my rock. I couldn't imagine life without him in it.

I'm still staring at the two-tiered dinosaur cake with red frosted lava flowing down the left side when a loud horn breaks into my thoughts. My head jerks up and my gaze travels to Zach.

"What was that?" I ask.

"Probably another moving van," he says. "There was one parked next door. The new neighbor is moving in."

The new neighbor is all anyone has talked about over the past week on our street. Rumor has it that Anne Graveley bought the house. She's a mystery author. Not uber famous, but she has had a couple successful novels. I am most curious about her.

"Talia!" Tabitha calls from the side yard. "I need help with these chairs."

The queen beckons and I run to her, as always.

TWO

TALIA

I put the last of the dishes into the dishwasher and slam the door shut. I glance over to my white granite kitchen island and smirk. Tabitha's right. Those PTA ladies really make that wine disappear. I grab the various bottles of pinot grigio and merlot and throw them into the trash receptacle. A quick wipe and my kitchen island is once again clean and clutter free.

Zach walks in from the backyard through the French doors. His nautical blue dress shirt sleeves are folded up to his elbows. He walks over and kisses me. A sweet kiss, but not a *let's get busy* kiss, which is good because right now I only want to get busy pulling on my pajamas.

"The backyard is all cleaned up," he says. "Grant took all his extra chairs home."

I laugh. "Good. It turned out to be a good party. Cole had fun."

"Oh, yeah, definitely," Zach agrees. He lifts a bottle of pinot hidden behind his back. "Found this half-full bottle outside. Should we take care of it?"

"Wow, how did that survive around Tabitha's friends?"

Zach laughs and grabs two wine glasses from one of our

antique white kitchen cabinets. I was very into the cleanness of crisp white when we remodeled the house. The kitchen has all white cabinets with gray accents on the cabinet handles, backsplash, and flooring. The large adjoining family room boasts more gray hardwood flooring, a large white marble fireplace and a large white sectional sofa, punctuated with solid gray and striped gray pillows. Neutral colors calm me.

We take our wine and sit on the sofa, propping our feet up on the, surprise, antique white coffee table: a large rectangle with beveled sides and beautiful curved legs. Perfect for a charcuterie board of goodies on movie night, or to eat our dinner on some nights. I take a big gulp of wine. The sweet nectar feels good sliding down my throat. I haven't had any all evening. I was too busy running around doing Tabitha's bidding.

"I'm just having one glass," says Zach. "I have to get up early tomorrow."

"Right, you're golfing with Jim tomorrow."

"Yeah, he wants to talk about this new loan promotion the bank is running next month," he replies.

I nod and take another sip of wine. Zach is the manager of a bank branch in Little Beak, but the main office is in Manhattan, where Jim is Vice President. Jim often combines their business talk with golfing, and Zach is more than happy to oblige.

"Is Grant joining you?" I ask. Sometimes, if they golf on the weekend, he does. Grant works on Wall Street and is in the city during the workday, but weekends he's usually game to hit the course.

"No, he had plans." Zach shakes his head. "Do you think something's going on with him?"

"Like what?"

"I don't know. He just seems kind of secretive sometimes."

"Secretive, how?"

"Like today, he was on his phone so much during Cole's party. I came into the house to get something, and he was in here texting. I surprised him and he shoved his phone into his pocket. It was so weird."

"Tabitha hasn't mentioned anything," I say. I glide my hand over his. "Not every couple can be as open as we are. It's special."

Zach smiles at me. "We do have something special. Do you think it's because we've known each other since we were six years old?"

I laugh. "Might have something to do with it. You can't hide anything from me. I know all your secrets."

"And vice versa." His warm brown eyes gaze into mine. "Maybe I'm imagining it with Grant. Something has just seemed off lately."

"You never know what's going on in other people's lives," I say. "If something is up with him, I'm sure we'll find out soon. Tabitha's not one for keeping secrets."

Zach smirks and places his empty wine glass on the coffee table. "Well, I'm tired. I'm going to bed. You coming?"

"You go ahead." I hold up the almost empty wine bottle. "This has another glass left."

"OK, enjoy." He kisses me goodnight. "I love you."

"I love you too." I smile, watching him walk up the wide, open, white-spindled stairway to our bedroom upstairs.

I pour the last of the pinot grigio into my glass. I glance at the French doors, noticing they're unlocked, and decide to check out the backyard for anything Zach may have overlooked. Instead of the wine making me sleepy, it's given me a mini burst of energy.

I step out onto the back patio. The comfortable gray and white striped patio chairs are neatly placed around the large tempered glass table with a bright red umbrella. I include a few pops of color here and there. The umbrella is still open. I go to crank the umbrella closed when a sudden movement along the thick bushes at the side yard catches my eye. I freeze and listen.

The bushes still. A faint scratching and then a loud thump on the other side of the bushes pierces the otherwise quiet night. Another thump. Louder this time. I creep over to the side yard and listen for a few moments. Silence. I move closer to the line of mature bushes that separate us from the house next door, and I peer through the small hole where one bush has decayed and dead limbs lend an unobstructed view of the neighbor's house. Now the new neighbor's.

She's outside, the new neighbor. The mystery author. Standing in her side yard, she is illuminated by the motion detector lights installed by the previous owners. She wears ratty-looking dark sweatpants and a hot pink long-sleeve T-shirt with a bright yellow lightning bolt on the front. Odd, in my opinion. I'd think a writer would choose more neutral tones, like me. But even odder is that she's standing there. Just standing there. Her gaze turns in my direction. I curl back, my heart beating fast, still able to see her; but, hopefully, she can't see me. Although, I'm not sure why I'm hiding from her. I'm not even sure why I'm spying on her. Another thump. Oh, that's why.

She stares for what seems like an eternity, then turns, and her long, dark curly hair in a high ponytail bounces against her neck. I move my face slightly deeper into the bushes to see where she has gone. She disappears from my view, then suddenly appears again, rounding the corner of her back porch, now carrying a large black trash bag, heading toward the drive-way, directly in my view. She moves like a freaking gazelle.

My skin pricks and the air around me seems stifled even though it's a crisp September evening. She is only taking out the garbage. Big deal. But was she snooping around in my yard earlier? Scoping out her new surroundings. Maybe even watching Zach and I through the glass doors? Something has been hiding in these bushes. Could a person hide inside of them? I never considered the question, but upon inspection, certain sections, like where I stand now, could accommodate a small person and give adequate cover to keep them hidden inside. A thought enters my mind, but I quickly dismiss it.

I just want to go back into my house, lock the door and get into bed with Zach. But now I'm stuck. If I start moving, she might see me. I stay as still as I possibly can, reminding me of the old game of Statue Tabitha and I used to play as children. Ugh... I never should have come outside. I'm trapped in my own yard.

Maybe I should brazen it out, walk over and introduce myself. But it's almost midnight. What kind of wacko introduces themselves to a new neighbor in the middle of the night?

A loud screech diverts both of our attention. The bushes to the right of me shake violently, and I clamp my hand over my mouth to stop any sound from slipping out. A fat orange cat emerges and runs over to my new neighbor, meowing loudly.

"Oh, there you are, Gilbert." She bends down and scoops him up. "You had me worried."

She pets the well-fed feline and the two disappear on their back porch. I hear a sliding glass door shut and the lock engage.

I let out a sigh of relief and sink down into the grass. The cat is hiding in my bushes and the neighbor is taking out the trash and looking for her cat. I laugh. Not exactly a reason to panic. Maybe I should start writing mystery novels. I certainly have the wild imagination. Tomorrow, I will properly introduce myself and take her a box of assorted cupcakes. And I won't mention I was spying on her through the bushes. I stand and brush the grass off my pants. I go back over to the umbrella, close it, give the yard a quick once-over; everything else looks in order. I yawn. Time for bed now.

A silver glint catches my eye before I turn to go inside the house. I walk over to the large planter, bursting with purple and white impatiens at the left side of the stone patio, and bend down to pick it up.

The object is a slim silver pen. It's from a popular hotel in

Manhattan. I finger the smooth pen and slip it into the pocket of my sweater. One of the guests must have lost it at the party. Odd, though, that Zach or I hadn't noticed it earlier, but not impossible. I stand at the exact spot the pen lay and turn toward the house. A direct view of the sofa where Zach and I drank our wine only a short time ago. The empty bottle still sits on the coffee table.

The cool night air chills me again. I glance over at the bushes once more, wondering if the neighbor was watching me. Watching us. I pull my sweater close to my body and go inside the house, securely locking the door.

THREE

TALIA

The warm September sun warms my face, a welcome departure from the previous chilly evening. I ponder my ridiculous behavior from last night and chalk it up to the wine. Today, in only a few minutes, I'll welcome the new neighbor properly. We will.

Tabitha walks in step beside me. A vision in a black, long-sleeve sheath dress with stylish gladiator sandals. Perhaps dressed more as if attending a funeral than visiting a new member of the Little Beak community. Why she would choose a dress like that for a casual visit is beyond me, but my mind doesn't work like Tabitha's. She likes to put on a show and have all eyes on her, always the belle of the ball. Nevertheless, she looks impeccable, as she always does.

We're identical twins, but there are always some differences. A scar on Tabitha's left ankle from a bike accident when she was ten. A cluster of moles on my right shoulder. Our bodies are different too. Tabitha is lean, every inch toned. I'm much more curvy, not overweight, but I like to eat the cakes I decorate from time to time and, crucially, don't dedicate two hours every day to Pilates and the gym.

Mostly, though, the difference lies in our personalities. Tabitha is the assertive leader. That was always her role, which left me the follower. Funny how we fell into those roles as children, yet as adults we continue to play them. Sure, we've matured, married, and live grownup lives, but those old conditions still apply, as strong at age thirty-two as eight years old. I didn't used to resent my role, but lately I've felt myself itching for more independence from my sister. I like the feeling. Pulling away from her makes me feel strong. Maybe pulling away is a bit harsh, let's say establishing boundaries. I've been taking more time for myself. I try not to immediately respond to Tabitha's calls or texts like I used to do. Small steps, but my independence builds with these simple choices. I'm proud of myself.

I clutch the pink bakery box with Little Beak Sweets written in swirly white letters on top. Inside are a dozen assorted cupcakes I hope our new friend will enjoy.

"Do you think she's home?" Tabitha asks. She brushes a long honey-gold lock of hair from her face.

"We will find out soon," I reply.

Tabitha nods and stares at me. "What are you wearing? You look like a librarian."

I look down to my pale peach sweater set, khaki pants and beige flats. "I do?"

"Nobody wears sweater sets anymore. We'll have to go shopping soon. Update your wardrobe a bit."

I give her a tight smile. Whatever. I like sweater sets. I own several.

We travel up the three steps on the front porch and approach the wide, ruby red door with a large brass doorknocker in the center. Two massive redwood planters flank the door, bright red petunias and green vinca vines spilling out of them. The former neighbors left them behind and I have been watering them daily.

Tabitha whispers before I rap the doorknocker, "I don't want to stay long."

"OK, a quick visit," I say, using the knocker. "Kind of exciting, though. Meeting an author."

"Oh, I don't know," Tabitha says. "The wife of a guy Grant works with is an author. For children though. She's not that great."

I nod. *I'm sure the children's author doesn't think you're that great either.*

Footsteps travel to the door. A pause. Then, the door swings open.

She stands there, the woman I spied on last night. Her thick, dark curly hair hangs wild around her slim shoulders. Wide-set, green eyes peer inquisitively at us through dark brown, tortoise-shell-style glasses, with a subtle glittery shimmer in the obviously expensive frames. Gone is the lightning bolt shirt, replaced with a white eyelet Henley and faded jeans. Hot pink flip-flops adorn her feet. Matching hot pink polish on her toenails. Wow, this chick really likes hot pink. I can already sense Tabitha assessing her. I wonder if hot pink ranks in the same column as sweater sets.

"Hello," she says.

"Hello," Tabitha greets warmly. She's a fine actress. I've seen her performance my entire life. She smiles broadly. "We're your new neighbors; we wanted to introduce ourselves."

She smiles. "You two must be related. The similarities are obvious."

Tabitha laughs. "Oh, yes, we're sisters. Twins."

I hand her the cupcake box. "I'm Talia Conner; I live next door. And my sister is Tabitha Norton; she lives next door to me. It's so lovely to meet you. We brought you a few cupcakes from our bakery in town. Hope you enjoy them."

"Oh, thank you." She accepts the box and smiles again. "I'm Anne. Anne Graveley."

"Oh, the writer," Tabitha gushes. "That must be an exciting job."

Anne's smile lessens, eyeing Tabitha. "It has its moments. Would you ladies like to come in? Have some coffee? And a cupcake?"

Tabitha opens her mouth to refuse, but I cut her off. "We'd love to, Anne."

Anne leads us inside and we follow her to the kitchen. The house looks the same as when the Edwards lived here. The older retired couple decided to move into a retirement community in sunny Florida for their golden years. They lived in this house for over thirty years and did little to update it as the years passed. Same wall paint, same carpet, same tile floor in the kitchen. Even some of the furniture and pictures on the wall are the same.

"Um." Tabitha pauses, obviously noticing the same as me. "I guess you have a lot of updating to do."

"Oh, I probably won't," Anne says. She walks over to a state-of-the-art coffee machine that probably could rival any coffee drink made at Starbucks and pours three mugs for each of us. Next time I'm asking for an espresso or a latte. Its chrome and black sleekness looks out of place among honey oak cabinets and plain laminate kitchen counter from the 1990s. "I'm only going to be here for a year."

"You bought a house to keep for a year?" I ask, confused.

"No, I'm renting it from the Edwards," she explains.

"Oh, I was certain this home was for sale," Tabitha says. Her hazel eyes spark with curiosity. "How did you end up renting it?"

"It was," explains Anne. "But the offers were lower than the Edwards expected. I contacted the realtor about renting and they were interested. The realtor thinks the sellers' market will be much better in a year or so. So this arrangement made the most sense for all of us."

"Interesting." Tabitha sits down at the oval oak kitchen table and takes a sip of coffee. "Ooh, this is really good."

"I don't skimp on coffee," Anne replies. "I live on the stuff." She opens the cupcake box now sitting on the table. "Which one should I choose?"

"My favorite is the raspberry filled chocolate," I say. "Salted caramel is a close second."

"Cookies and cream for me," Tabitha says. "When I indulge myself. And occasionally the raspberry filled chocolate. It's hard not to love that combination."

The large orange cat from last night emerges from the doorway and walks into the kitchen, meowing profusely.

"Oh, hello, Gil... kitty!" I correct myself. How would I know his name was Gilbert unless I admit watching her last night?

Tabitha and Anne both look at me in a peculiar fashion.

Anne picks up the cat. "This is Gilbert. He probably thinks he's going to get a cupcake, but he's wrong." She strokes his fur and gives him a nuzzle before placing him back on the floor. She surveys the cupcake selection again. "I'm going with the salted caramel." She offers the box. "What are you having?"

I politely pluck a raspberry filled chocolate, but Tabitha declines.

"Just coffee for me." She waves her hand. "So, why did you rent this relic from the nineties for a year?"

Anne takes a bite of the cupcake and wipes the frosting from her mouth. She chews and swallows, lending a long pause before answering the question. I can see the telltale signs that Tabitha is irritated by her slow response. Tabitha taps her fingers on the table and purses her lips together. My anxiety rises, never quite sure of Tabitha's reactions in social situations. She can be unpredictable.

"Well," she says, taking her time. "First, this cupcake is delicious. Second, I'm here to write a new manuscript. Three, in fact. I'm working on a trilogy."

"How exciting," I say, taking a sip of coffee. "More mysteries?"

"Yes, these take place in a fictional town very similar to Little Beak. I want to immerse myself in the town and really get a feel for it. Plus, I was craving a quiet location. I needed a break from the city. As much as I enjoy the hustle and bustle, a quiet pause is welcome too."

"Sure, that sounds wonderful." Tabitha nods. She looks at me. "Well, sis, we really should go. I'm sure Anne has a lot of unpacking to do."

"Not that much," Anne says. "The Edwards left most of the furniture. I only brought my bed, desk, clothes, and coffee machine." She laughs. "Keeping it simple."

"That's great. Simple isn't really my thing, but I'm glad it works so well for you. So nice to meet you, Anne." Tabitha stands and walks toward the front door. "Thank you for the coffee."

"Yes, wonderful to meet you." I smile at her. "Maybe we can do lunch sometime? There's a cute café down from our bakery. They have great wraps and soups."

"I'd love to," Anne agrees, following us to the door. She waves as we walk down the sidewalk. "Thanks for stopping in and for the delicious cupcakes!"

We wave and smile back, walking silently until we're out of Anne's sight, just past the bush hedge I hid behind last night. The way Tabitha walks shows her agitation. I'm certain I'll be soon hearing about whatever is the source of the tension and her hasty departure from Anne's house. I follow behind her.

"We're going to my house," Tabitha hisses under her breath. "I have to tell you something."

"OK," I mumble. What is going on with her now? Something with Anne set her off during the brief visit, although I can't imagine what since I thought the visit was quite pleasant.

· · ·

We walk down the sidewalk, past my charming red brick two-story colonial style three-bedroom home with pearl white shutters and a modest front yard, bursting with mounds of colorful flower beds: Zach's handiwork, not mine. Our two-car attached garage sits to the left at the end of a generous paved driveway. Mature hedges outline our half-acre property. A few steps away, tall, majestic sugar maple and chestnut oak trees line each side of Grant and Tabitha's one-acre property. The jewel of the street.

Their home, a very generous wedding gift from Grant's parents, reminds me of the house in the *Home Alone* movie. Large, gracious three-story, five-bedroom home with two charming dormers on the top floor. Red brick, Georgian style with black shutters and more mature trees in the front yard.

It sits back further from the street than the other homes in the area, and it has vibrant flower beds around the house and numerous islands in the yard to add color: their gardener, Louis's, handiwork. An expansive, detached three-car garage, with an apartment loft above it that our parents use when visiting us, sits even farther back on the property, starting toward the back of the house, a long driveway leading to its entrance.

We scurry up the driveway and enter through the laundry room at the side of the house. Cool air conditioning welcomes us as we walk inside. I don't realize how warm I am until that refreshing air cools my skin. It may be September, but the summer heat is in full force in Little Beak.

"First, I'm taking off this stupid dress!" Tabitha yells. She rips off her gladiator sandals and unzips the dress, flinging it on a bench next to the dryer. She grabs a light blue cotton robe from a peg shelf to the side of the washer. "I was sweating like a pig in it."

"Why did you wear that anyway? It's warm today and it has

long sleeves. No wonder you're sweating. You always get warm in long sleeves."

"It's Christian Dior, that's why."

"Who cares? Don't forget we grew up wearing Walmart clothes. Don't act like you're some trust fund baby."

"Don't ever say that again, especially in front of people." She points a finger at me. "What do you know? You're wearing a sweater set!"

I sigh. "Why did you want me here?"

Tabitha looks at me. "We've got big problems with this new neighbor."

"Why? Because she's not remodeling the Edwards' house?"

Tabitha shakes her head. "No. Look, something is going on with Grant. At work."

"OK, what?" I'm completely lost. What has that got to do with Anne?

"I'm not exactly sure, but he said he thinks there's moles, spies, at his firm. He said some of his bigger clients don't even want to take meetings at the office. They meet in hotels in the city instead."

"That doesn't sound right. The clients think something is going on too?"

"He's cryptic. I guess because he can't tell me everything, but something is going on and this writer, Anne, now moving into our neighborhood seems shady to me. What if she's here to spy on us? There's no way the Edwards didn't have offers on that house. The real estate market is booming."

Wow, she's way over the top on this one. "Why would an author be spying on a guy that works on Wall Street? Makes no sense. And how do you know the real estate market is booming? You don't even watch the news."

She frowns at me. "I just know. I've heard people talking about it. Don't you remember that TV show Mom used to watch, *Castle*? That guy was an author who worked with the police. It's possible."

"That's a TV show, not real life," I say, exasperated. But even so, I fumble around in my sweater pocket and pull out the silver pen I found on the patio last night. I hand it to Tabitha.

She stares at it. "A pen? From a hotel."

"I found it on my patio last night."

"And...?"

"Do you think it's Grant's or one of your friends' from the party?"

"Talia, I don't know. It's a free pen. Hotels give them away. It is a hotel Grant's mentioned going to though, just in case I saw it on the credit card statement."

"So, you think it's his?"

"I have no idea. Maybe. Keep it if you want. He's not going to miss a stupid pen."

"Okay." I slide the pen back into my pocket. "You know, Zach mentioned Grant was acting oddly lately."

"Really?" Tabitha smiles, her face softening. "Well, Zach is one of us. He knows us better than anyone."

"Do you think Grant is telling you everything?"

"No, he's not, but that's because he can't. I trust him." Her voice is soft. "I do."

Tabitha's weak spot has always been Grant. She will go the extra mile with him, if needed, and not many people fit in that category for her: I don't even always know if I do. Grant swept into her life, and she loves being consumed by him, craves it, unlike any relationship I've witnessed her in before. I remember her talking about this "hot guy" she was dating and, when I met Grant, I saw she was not exaggerating, for once. Not just good-looking, but, yes, a hot guy. Dark blond hair, ocean blue eyes, body sculpted by hours of gym time, an outgoing personality and great sense of humor. He had even modeled as a teenager. However, he's also closed off, distant at times and his own welfare almost always comes first. Not caring and compassionate like my Zach. On the surface he's incredibly polite, but when things get messy, he will disappear. He doesn't want to deal with issues when they become complicated. He'll throw money at a problem and hope it will go away. Tabitha doesn't see Grant's faults; I think it's because she too has similar qualities. She's always the bully in our relationship and when things get messy, leaves me, or Zach, to clean things up for her. I think of Grant and Tabitha as kindred spirits, but not necessarily in a good way. They may just be the perfect couple.

Anne as a spy to observe Grant though? Seems unlikely. Ludicrous even. Who would she be conducting surveillance for? I hate to think it, but Grant's story sounds like something he made up so that Tabitha wouldn't question hotel charges on their credit card. And if that's true, Tabitha better start doing some investigating of her own into Grant's activities. Some questions linger, though. Why *did* Anne Graveley choose our town to settle in for a year to write her books? If I was a writer, I'd pick a waterfront town by the ocean to lull away the days writing my novels. So many cozy towns like ours to choose from in the general area. Why Little Beak? Why now?

FOUR

TABITHA

I watch Talia walk across my driveway, through the tree line and back over to her house. Or maybe she'll stop in with her new friend, Anne, to apologize for her rude sister. She's been doing things like that since we were kids. I didn't choose the position, but it is the part I have to play; the only one who understands the importance of what I do for her is Zach. He sees how I step up when I need to, when Talia needs me to be the strong sister.

Talia, the perfect, polite one who follows me around everywhere. I'm always the one who jumps ahead and makes sure the path is clear for myself and for her. I'm always the one who takes care of the messy stuff, and I'm the one who gets hurt; but nobody ever seems to care if my feelings are bruised.

I cringe thinking about Talia's comment about us wearing Walmart clothes. Not that it isn't true, it is, but that's the last thing I need for people to hear around this neighborhood and especially not around Grant's blue blood family. She better keep her mouth shut with those kinds of comments. By now she should know comments like that hurt me. I maintain a certain type of lifestyle and I help her to do the same. Our past is behind us, and I will not look in the rearview mirror.

The robe I am wearing, although comfortable, is thin and I go upstairs to our bedroom to find something else to put on. Yes, I showed off for Anne by wearing the designer dress. I can be a bitch sometimes; I fully admit it. Big deal.

Our bed is unmade. The housekeeper is off sick today. I could make it, but I don't want to. I take off my robe and fling it on the cream club chair next to our sleigh-style bed with sumptuous one thousand thread count sheets. I'm tempted to crawl into my bed and take a little nap, but I continue to my walk-in closet, the crème de la crème of closets. Basically, the best closet I've ever encountered. I fling open the double doors and marvel at the rows of neatly hanging dresses in many hues, pants and skirts, sweaters nestled in compartments ahead of me and various tops and blazers in all shades. A section to the left houses my purses, another array of various colors, giving me many choices depending on my outfit. At the end of my dress row my collection of shoes, boots, and sandals is positioned neatly on a rotating carousel. None are from Walmart.

I lie down on the periwinkle-colored chaise lounge in the center of the closet. I never could have imagined a closet like this growing up in our modest farmhouse upstate. Talia and I shared a bedroom. We didn't have to, strictly speaking, except for the year we were fifteen, because there was an extra bedroom, but we liked sharing a room. Plus, we used the extra room as a play area, and Mom liked having a guest bedroom when our grandparents came to visit.

We were far from rich. And now, looking back at the life I lived, it almost seems like a dream. Or a nightmare. Worry snakes through me, especially after my conversation with Grant. I can say I'm sick with worry, but that makes me sound pathetic. But I don't want anything to change in my life. Grant has given me a fairy tale, just as I hoped. And I feel sure that

Anne poses a threat to it. To our way of life. Mine, Grant's, Talia's and Zach's. Talia is always oblivious to threats; she never sees the underlying darkness in people like I do. I'm the one who takes care of her while she skips around with her sunshine grin and does whatever she wants, despite my feelings. Everything I did for her in the past was to protect her, to protect us and our special relationship. Twins are different from other siblings. Twins stay together. She's never realized how much I've sacrificed for her.

And she never will.

FIVE

TALIA

Cole bites into his second slice of pepperoni pizza, sauce dripping down his cherubic face. I snatch a napkin and hand it to him.

"You might need this," I say, turning my attention back to my own slice of pizza.

He laughs, a sweet child's laugh, and wipes away the offending sauce, then takes another big bite of pizza. We sit on wide bar stools at the large, black quartz center island in Tabitha and Grant's massive Shaker gray kitchen. High-end appliances, including a Sub-Zero refrigerator, marble backsplash, and a crystal chandelier as a lighting fixture above the island are a few highlights of the impressive room.

Tabitha and Grant are going to a charity function tonight in Manhattan and will be staying overnight. I will stay at their house to babysit Cole. Pizza, video games, movie and lights out at 9 p.m. I'll have a fun evening with my nephew. I always enjoy spending time with him.

The week passed without incident. We are busy in the bakery, cakes for two princess parties and Marge's retirement party at the bank, plus a large cupcake order for the local Mercedes dealership doing a customer appreciation celebration. Foot traffic has been steady too. I'm glad we hired Claire, one of our other neighbors down the street, to help in the shop. Having another person to ring up orders and take care of customers is a great help. She had been a stay-at-home mom, but her daughter is now in first grade and Claire was looking for a part-time job. The arrangement works perfectly for all of us. The week was satisfying and enjoyable. And tonight, I'm happy to spend time with my favorite nephew.

I haven't seen Anne since the day Tabitha and I visited. I still feel curious about her, and I'm embarrassed to admit, I even watched through the bushes once or twice, wondering if I'd see anything interesting. I found another opening in the bushes, farther back into our yard, where I could see her back porch. It was a bit thicker than the other hole, so I got out the garden shears and trimmed it until the view was clear yet provided enough cover for me to remain hidden. The only thing I observed was one evening I heard music playing and the low hum of conversation mixed with glasses clinking, and the clang of silverware against plates wafting through an open window. However, nobody emerged from the house, at least on my watch and, oddly, no cars were parked in the driveway. Anne obviously had company, but it must have been someone local who walked to her home. I found that puzzling since she just moved in. Did she already know people in the neighborhood? Is that why she moved here?

Nevertheless, having company over and playing music in her house wasn't exactly evidence of being a spy or anything strange, just a regular person. Tabitha's insistence that Anne is up to something involving Grant probably is based off jealousy; I don't know why I didn't recognize it right away. Anne is clearly an attractive woman and Tabitha doesn't like it, plain and simple. I promise myself I will stop observing her secretly and follow through on inviting her to lunch next week. Without Tabitha.

"How's that pizza?" Grant asks as he and Tabitha enter the kitchen.

He wears a well-tailored tuxedo and she a stunning silver evening gown. Delicate diamond pendant earrings hang from her earlobes, and a gorgeous diamond necklace adorns her neck. They look like Ken and Barbie going out for a night on the town. Smashing.

"It's so good, Dad!" Cole exclaims. "Aunt Talia and I are going to play video games after we eat!"

"Oh, that sounds fun, buddy," Grant replies, smiling at his son.

"You two look amazing," I say.

"Of course we do," Tabitha says with her usual confidence. "This is a huge event, especially for Grant's mother."

Grant's mother is overseeing the fundraiser for cancer research. She has spearheaded this particular division of the charity for the past ten years. Since both her parents died of cancer, fundraising for a cure is of great importance to her. Grant's parents are old New York money, firmly entrenched in New York society and all of its various social gatherings. I don't think I would embrace all the social functions involved with such a standing, but Tabitha slipped right into that role. She enjoys any excuse to buy a fancy new dress and parade around with her good-looking husband.

"Have a good time!" I say, cheerfully, hugging Cole. "Don't worry about us. We're going to have lots of fun."

"Thanks, Talia." Grant smiles. "We appreciate it."

"Yes, we do," Tabitha says. "You know I wish you and Zach would hurry up and have a baby soon, so Cole has a cousin to play with."

So do we. A year ago her off-hand comment would have probably made me cry, but tonight it bounces off me, only a prick of hurt, quickly dissolving. She's insensitive, always has been, and I have to deal with my own feelings and not allow her to bring me down.

"That would be nice," I reply.

"Babe, we really have to go," Grant says, giving Cole a high five. "Be good for Aunt Talia. We'll be back tomorrow."

"Bye, Mom. Bye, Dad," Cole chirps.

Tabitha kisses the top of his blond head. "Bye, sweetie." She looks at me. "Thanks, Talia."

They leave and Cole and I finish our pizza. Between bites I think about Tabitha and how hurtful she can be. We are so different. Yet, she can be very generous, too. Grant as well. She and Grant had lived in their home for about a year when the house next door went up for sale. Zach and I still lived in a small town upstate, not far from our parents, and Tabitha had been hounding us to move closer to them. Zach was working as a branch manager at a local bank, and I worked in a bookstore. We couldn't afford a house in this area on our salary, but Tabitha and Grant made it happen. They gave us the down payment for our house, plus a little extra, and Grant secured the bank manager position for Zach at a substantially higher salary than he was making at his old job. Grant's father is a good friend of the bank president. Tabitha was already baking and selling cupcakes from her home. Baking and fancy cake decorating was something we'd enjoyed doing together since we were young girls. So two years later, we opened the shop in town. Whatever Tabitha wants, Tabitha gets. I hold a love/hate feeling for this fact. On one hand, I admire how she goes after what she wants, despite the difficulty it may take to obtain it, but on the other hand, I hate how she always gets what she wants and I feel like I trail along, picking up her crumbs. I suppose I'll always have conflicted feelings about Tabitha. I know if I ever stand in the way of what she wants, I will not stand a chance.

"Aunt Talia, video game time," Cole says, smiling.

"OK, let's go." I deposit our dishes in the dishwasher. Then Cole and I go on our video game quest.

The evening passes quickly and pleasantly. Cole is a great kid and I enjoy spending time with him. Before I know it, I'm tucking a very sleepy boy into his bed.

"Goodnight, Cole," I say, kissing his forehead.

"Night." His voice trails off. He rolls over on his right side and snuggles into his pillow. I watch him for a few moments and pat his soft blond head. He's so sweet and loving. I hope I have a child one day. Maybe we should investigate IVF. It isn't a road I'm ready to take yet. I still have the feeling Zach and I will make a baby the old-fashioned way. It just isn't our time, yet.

A thump outside breaks into my thoughts. I turn and listen. Another thump and the neighbor's dog barks. I go to the window and pull back Cole's dark blue dinosaur curtains and peer outside. A harvest moon hangs high in the night sky, its light illuminating a dark clothed figure walking up the stairs to the apartment above Grant and Tabitha's garage.

Fear spreads through me. What the hell? Who is that? I watch the figure, diminutive in size, so I assume it is a woman, or a very slight man, move agilely up the stairs to the apartment. The figure wears dark sweatpants, possibly yoga pants, and a long dark sweatshirt with the hood pulled up, not revealing any clue of hair or face. They continue to move fast up the stairs, turn the knob, and go inside. I stare, my mind filling with questions.

Doesn't Tabitha usually keep that door locked? My heart races. Who would want to break into the apartment? Should I go outside and confront the person? What if they have a weapon? I glance at Cole, still sleeping soundly in his bed, and tiptoe out of his room, softly closing the door behind me.

I race downstairs silently, grabbing the extra keys Tabitha

gave me earlier, lying on the kitchen counter, and fly out to the dark laundry room at the back of the house. It faces the garage and apartment.

I still for a moment, by the dryer, debating on whether to go outside and confront the person or just hide and watch. If Zach was home, I'd call him, but he's at a poker game night at a friend's house across town. It will take him too long to get here. I should let him know that something's up though; in case anything happens to me, someone needs to be here for Cole. I pull my phone out of the pocket in my leggings and tap out a text to Zach. I spy a baseball bat propped up in a corner of the laundry room from Cole's Little League team. I grab it and open the door, then lock it behind me with the key I had grabbed from the counter in case the intruder decides to try the house.

I can't go far. Cole's inside so I have to stay close. I keep my eyes on the apartment to be sure nobody emerges. I need something to camouflage my presence. I don't want to confront the trespasser with only a baseball bat: If he or she has a gun, no contest on who will win that fight. No lights are turned on, but a dim moving light bobs through the space. A flashlight.

There aren't many places to hide. I choose a large forsythia bush midway to the apartment entrance. I wait, my breath sounding louder than it ever has in my life. My heart thumps so loudly in the quiet night I fear the intruder may hear it once they leave the apartment. I silently try to calm myself. Questions flood my mind. Why would someone want to break into the apartment? Why wasn't it locked? The moonlight streams down, bright tonight, and I have a decent view of the apartment steps. I peer from the right side of the massive shrubbery. The door opens and the hooded figure exits. Their head hangs down, face obscured. I flatten myself as much as possible, but still can view the stranger through an opening in the bush. They are wearing yoga pants. Most definitely a woman. She moves fast down the stairs and takes off across the driveway.

I follow her as she disappears into the row of trees lining the property. The interloper slows after she passes them. I stand behind a wide oak and watch her trot out onto the sidewalk, disappearing. I want to follow her but I can't leave Cole alone. I sigh, walk across the driveway, and head upstairs to the dark apartment.

I turn the knob and open the door. I flick on the light switch, illuminating the room. Nothing appears disturbed. The living room area combo with a small kitchen is still neat and tidy. A comfortable leather sofa, matching recliner, and a small round kitchen table, covered in a bright yellow tablecloth, occupy the room. Even the throw blankets on the sofa are tightly folded and hanging over the back, pillows properly arranged. It isn't a space I'm often inside, usually only when our parents visit, and even then, for very short periods of time.

I walk across the wood laminate flooring into the bedroom at the back of the apartment. I click on the light in the room and the one in the adjoining bathroom. I do a quick check of the small bathroom space. Pretty basic, shower, toilet, vanity with a sink. I hesitate but then pull back the white eyelet shower curtain. Nothing out of place to my eye, thank God. I would have a heart attack if someone jumped out at me. I go back to the bedroom. A queen-size bed, with a powder blue quilt and matching pillow shams sits in the center of the room, the quilt rumpled in the center. Pillows in the center of the bed were also moved and rumpled. Was the woman lying on the bed? That's weird.

Something is lying on the floor, half hidden under the bed quilt. I bend down and retrieve the small item. I stare at it. A black hair barrette with a delicate pink daisy. Hot pink.

SIX

TALIA

On Sunday morning, Zach and I eat omelets and drink coffee at Tabitha's kitchen island. Cole has already eaten, and he left shortly after ten. His friend Tyler's mother picked him up to go to Sunday School with them and, afterward, a church picnic.

I called Tabitha last night and told her everything about the break-in. She was upset and wanted to come home right away, but Grant talked her out of it. I assured her things were fine now and Zach was staying over with me and Cole.

"More coffee?" I ask Zach, holding the carafe.

"Sure," he says.

I fill his mug. A key turns in the laundry room door and opens. Grant and Tabitha walk into the kitchen.

Tabitha paces around the kitchen island, a blur in white leggings and a comfortable-looking red tunic, her breathing heavy: agitation covers her face as soon as she enters the house.

"Someone broke into our apartment. Why didn't you stop them and call the police?"

"Well..." I stumble, shooting Zach a glance. "I didn't know if they had a weapon."

"No, you were right, Talia," Grant interjects, coming up

behind her. He stands in front of Tabitha, blocking her path, so she'll stop walking in a circle. "We're happy that everyone is okay."

Tabitha huffs at him and turns the opposite way. She pulls open the door to the refrigerator and stares at its contents, then slams the door shut. She turns to us. "It's just such an invasion. We must call the police."

"I agree," Zach says. "What if this person comes back?"

Grant shrugs. "I don't think they will."

Zach glares at him. "You don't *think* they will? Your family could be in danger."

Tabitha grabs her cell phone. "I'm calling the police. Zach is right. What if this person comes back when Cole is playing outside? Or they try to get into the house?"

Grant takes her phone. "Let's sleep on it, honey. It's too fresh right now."

Tabitha glares at him and snatches her phone back. Zach and I share a glance.

"I think we are going to go home," I say. "Let us know if you need anything."

They both nod and we show ourselves to the door.

"What is going on with Grant?" I say to Zach when we are out of earshot. "He was acting like it was no big deal."

"He's being an idiot," Zach fumes. "He *is* an idiot!"

We walk back to our house in silence the rest of the way. My nerves are frazzled, but I feel it is only the beginning of something unsettling brewing in Little Beak.

Later, in the afternoon, Tabitha texts me, upset that Grant won't budge on calling the police.

> Why wouldn't he want to report a break in at our house?

> I don't know

> What do you think? Wouldn't you and Zach call the police?

I consider for a moment. Probably. As upset as Zach is about the incident, I know he would report it. Another text pops up from Tabitha.

> Grant's solution is to install a new security system.

> Well, that's good, right? Hey, come over. I have something to show you.

Three dots.

I wait, but no response appears. I get up to use the bathroom. When I return to the sofa, one unread message is on my phone.

> I'll be there in ten minutes.

In the evening, at dinner, Zach and I sit at our dining room table eating lasagna I prepared and a salad he prepared. Both taste delicious, but our conversation is getting on my nerves. I take another bite of lasagna and try to tune out Zach's rantings, which have gone on for hours. I want to move to another subject.

"I don't understand," he says, stabbing his salad with a fork. "Why isn't he more upset. Why isn't he doing something?"

"What's he going to do?" I ask, taking a sip of water.

"Go to the police. Something." Zach's brow furrows. Irritation colors his face. "What if this person tries to hurt Cole or Tabitha? They were obviously creeping around for something. What if they didn't find it and they come back?"

"I agree Grant's reaction was odd," I say. "But I don't think anyone's in any physical danger."

"You don't know that." Zach shakes his head. "And I still can't believe you chased them. You could have been hurt." He rises from his seat and rounds the table, giving me a hug. I lean into him for a moment. "That's why I'm so upset by this." He walks back to his seat.

"I had a baseball bat," I remind him.

"Yeah, real helpful if they have a gun," he says sarcastically.

Grant's reaction to the stranger at the apartment is undoubtedly odd. I wonder if his underrated reaction is due to something he knows but we do not. Something having to do with his shady work issues? None of this story makes sense. When Tabitha came over this afternoon, she was even more certain Anne had something to do with the break-in, and I didn't rule out the possibility. I showed her the daisy barrette I'd found on the floor, and she made me swear not to tell Grant. I wanted to keep the barrette, but Tabitha insisted on keeping it. Since it was on her property, I had to let it go.

Zach is still outraged about it. It's all I have heard about since Grant and Tabitha arrived home and we discussed it briefly with them. I'm glad I called Tabitha to let her know about the incident, but also glad it didn't ruin their evening. There was no need to rush home that night. We were fine. I called Zach and he stayed with me and Cole. Now, Sunday evening and he is still harping on about it. I am sick of his ranting and raving. Sometimes he can be incredibly obsessive.

"I mean if that happened to us, I'd do everything I could to keep you safe," he says. "I told you something was going on with Grant."

"They are putting a new state-of-the-art alarm system in the house, garage and apartment. Upgrading everything," I reply. "That's something."

"Not much," Zach sighs. "It makes me mad. I don't want anyone to get hurt."

"Can we talk about something else?" I ask, irritated. "This is all we've been talking about for the last day and a half."

Zach shakes his head again. "I can't believe you aren't more upset." He pushes his food away and stands up. "She is *your* sister." He stomps upstairs.

I sigh, staring at his half-eaten plate of lasagna. It has been a while since one of Zach's erratic outbursts. As kind and compassionate as he is, he also has an unstable edge that explodes from time to time. He'll be back to normal in a day or two. I hope.

I don't disagree with him, but I am sick of analyzing the situation. Grant and Tabitha are grownups; they can make their own decisions. Yes, something strange is going on, no doubt. Eventually we'll get answers. I only want to focus on my own next steps.

The barrette is the only clue. If I find the owner, I'll know who was sneaking around in the apartment. The first step is inviting Anne to lunch. I'll stop by and ask her tomorrow. Tonight, I'll let Zach stew in his anger, however well intended.

I approach Anne's ruby red front door and engage the brass doorknocker. It feels a bit rude just stopping by again without calling. I need to get her cell number then I can simply text her, not randomly knock on her door all the time. I don't hear any movement inside the house. I look over to the bay window in the living room on the right of the house. A slight movement of the closed curtain reveals someone, or something watching me. I ring the doorbell this time. Footsteps. The door creaks open, and Anne stands there wearing pale yellow pajama bottoms and a black tank top.

"Oh, hey, Talia... I think?" she laughs.

"Right." I smile. "Yeah, sometimes it's hard to tell me and Tabitha apart in the beginning."

"Well, I don't think Tabitha would stop in on her own."

I laugh again. "I don't know. You might be surprised. Anyway, I wanted to see if you'd like to go out to lunch with me today. Maybe around twelve thirty?"

"Sure." She pauses. There is a noise in the back of the house, a scuffling. "I'm working on something now. But I'll see you then."

"Great, come over to my place. I'll drive," I offer. "One more thing, may I have your cell number? A lot easier to text you."

"I'll give it to you at lunch." She closes the door without a goodbye.

Well, that is abrupt. She did say she was busy, but still. I turn, go down the steps and walk back to my house. It is Monday, our day off. The bakery is open Tuesday through Friday nine till five, Saturday nine till two, closed Sunday and Monday. Most days I start work early, around eight; Claire comes in at nine and works until two; Tabitha usually comes in at eleven, but she always closes the shop. Mornings are busy for her, dropping Cole off at school and then the gym. She has her housekeeper pick Cole up at school and start dinner. Dinner is usually almost ready by the time she gets home; she likes it that way. I leave around three each day and hit the gym sometimes on the way home. Claire and I handle Saturdays for the most part. Tabitha comes in if I have plans. We all like the schedule.

I glance at my phone. Nothing from Zach. After his outburst last night, I was frosty with him this morning, and we barely spoke before he left for work. I regret it now. I just want him to shake off the obsession with Saturday night. I still have a couple hours until lunch with Anne. I change direction and head toward Tabitha's house. We can have coffee and chat if she is back from the gym. I amble through the shady tree line enjoying the fresh morning air. I'm a morning person. I enjoy being awake when others are still in deep slumber and the quiet peacefulness solitude brings to me. A fresh beginning of early morning sunshine with birds chirping and a soft warm breeze caressing my face makes me smile. I walk up the long paved driveway to Tabitha's house, then I stop. Grant walks out of the garage apartment and steps onto the stairs. I stare at him.

What is he doing home?

Why isn't he at work? I hesitate, wondering if I should turn around and go home. Grant lifts his head and sees me standing halfway up his driveway. He gives me an awkward wave. I can't turn around now. I wave back, just as awkwardly.

He's wearing blue gym shorts, a white tank top, and sneakers, his arm muscles rippling in perfect form. I wonder how many hours he spends at the gym lifting weights. I always find myself staring at him when he has little clothing on, like today—probably not a good idea. We walk toward each other and meet at the top of the driveway.

"Hey, Grant," I greet him in a cheerful voice. "What are you doing home?"

"Oh, I have an appointment later so just took the day off. Just getting ready to take a run," he says. "You here to see Tabitha?"

"Yeah, just thought I'd pop by. If she's busy, no big deal," I reply.

"She's not here." He clears his throat. "She went into the city to go shopping. With Lucy."

"Lucy?" I never heard of her.

"She's one of my sister's friends. It was a spur of the moment thing they planned at the charity dinner we went to on Saturday night."

"Oh, OK," I mumble. "Well, enjoy your day off. I'll catch up with Tabitha later."

"See you, Talia," he says, turning back up the driveway.

I can feel his eyes on me as I continue down the driveway to my house. Everything about this is off. Grant is hardly ever home alone on a weekday, especially if Tabitha's away. He usually only takes days off when they go on vacation. And it's unusual that Tabitha didn't mention an impromptu trip with this Lucy. Yes, there was a lot going on when we talked on Saturday, but still.

I hurry to our house and let myself in through the side door on the garage. I swear, thinking I probably should have locked it, but I only intended to pop over to Anne's and back home again. Now with all these odd occurrences I should keep the doors always locked.

I go into the kitchen and put a K-Cup into the Keurig to brew. While it gurgles, I think again about how odd it is that Grant is home, and why is he in the apartment? Probably just wanted to check it out again after what happened Saturday night. Still, something unsettles me.

The coffee stops pouring. I add a bit of cream and walk out onto my stone patio. The beautiful early autumn day once again welcomes me, but uneasiness stirs inside me. Why was Anne so abrupt when I invited her to lunch? She was friendly but it's obvious she wanted me to leave. What is she working on? Writing or did it have something to do with Grant?

I look at my tall green hedges not on Anne's side this time, but Tabitha's. I remember when we first moved here, I would stand on my tiptoes and look over them to see if Tabitha's car was in the driveway. Since their larger property sits back farther than ours, our backyard lines up to their garage and driveway. The hedges are much too tall now and I haven't done this for years.

I sit my coffee down on the patio table and walk all the way to the back of the yard. The hedges are thicker on this side, no opening with dead limbs. I try to clear a space with my hand but only get scratched in the process. I debate getting gardening shears from the garage to make my own hole like I did on the other side.

"What are you doing?" a voice asks.

I yelp and jump away from the hedge, my heart racing as if it will pound right out of my chest. I turn around.

Anne stands in my yard. She wears different clothing than when I visited her earlier. Now a lightweight mint-colored sweater and khaki shorts. Cute white sandals with a white daisy on the top encase her feet. A daisy.

She stares at me, a quizzical look covering her face. Her body language isn't hostile, but I feel intimidated. Why is she here?

"Oh, you surprised me," I squeak. I clear my throat. "Just looking at a bird nest."

She walks toward me. "Let me see it."

"No," I cut her off, walking directly at her. "I thought I saw a bird nest, but I was wrong."

Anne nods. "Funny how our imagination plays tricks on us."

"Yes," I agree. "So, what's up?"

"I felt a bit bad with how abrupt I'd been with you earlier," Anne explains. "Does this café also serve breakfast? I could really go for a good eggs Benedict. And maybe a bit of shopping afterward? And here"—she hands me her cell phone—"put your number in, then I'll call you and you'll have mine."

"Sure." I force a smile, adding my number to her phone. An uneasy sickness creeps into my stomach. "Let me get my purse."

SEVEN

TALIA

After the short drive to the café and settling into our seats, my uneasiness quickly dissipates. Over lattes we chat like old friends about everything ranging from favorite movies, books and how unathletic each of us is in every sport. The semi emptiness of the café is nice because we don't feel a need to rush and enjoy our conversation at a leisurely pace. We sit on the terrace at an oval table with a small, terracotta pot in the center containing a sprig of ivy, shaded by an emerald-green umbrella. A slight breeze ripples the dark green cloth napkins tucked under my plate.

The only other occupants of the terrace are two elderly women sitting on the opposite side. Large rectangular boxes line the railing around the space, spilling over with robust ivy leaves. We ask the waitress for refills on the lattes.

"This eggs Benedict is divine," Anne says, taking another bite. "How's your omelet?"

"Good." I take another bite. "So, are you all settled in now? How's the writing going?"

"Pretty much. I started working on my manuscript and it's flowing well."

"Oh, is that what you were working on earlier today?"

"Yes, I was working on a prologue and wanted to get it finished before doing anything else. When you have something specific in your mind, you must write it down."

"Makes sense," I say. "What is your book about?"

Anne smiles at me. "About a woman with a premonition that involves a friend. Kind of a life and death situation and many unknown factors play into the story."

"Ooh, I can't wait to read it," I say. "Sounds really interesting."

Anne nods. "Where do you want to shop today?"

"Honestly, I'd rather just sit here and chat for a bit. Would you mind if we went shopping another day?"

"I'd love that," says Anne.

"OK, great. I'm having such a nice time with you. I'm glad we did this."

Anne laughs. "I agree, probably better without Tabitha. She seems very... opinionated."

I look at her. "True."

"Do you come to the café often? It's really nice."

"Tabitha and I come here sometimes. And my husband likes to meet here for lunch. He loves their chicken salad wrap."

"Oh, yeah, he's the bank manager at the bank down the street, right?"

"Yes," I say, staring at her. "How did you know that?"

"It's a small town. He's a big fish. Well, all of you are big fish here."

"Really?"

"You and your husband, Tabitha and her husband. Kind of like Little Beak royalty."

I never heard this before, but I guess people talk.

"Wow, I didn't realize we were such a big deal," I say.

Anne laughs. She laughs a lot. Maybe too much. I'm starting to wonder if it is a performance.

"Oh, it's nothing," she replies, sipping her latte.

"It must be quite an adjustment living in Little Beak compared to Manhattan," I say, changing the subject.

She nods. "For sure. I always loved that you could get anything you want any time you want it in the city, but there are advantages here too."

"The quiet, the peacefulness, friendly people?" I suggest.

"Of course." A small smile forms on her full red lips. Her pale nails clutch the white coffee mug. "Among other things."

I settle into our king-sized bed, snuggling under the warm covers, pulling them up to my chin. I grab the remote and scroll through Netflix, looking for something to watch, settling on a romantic comedy. Something funny and light is exactly what I need to distract me from my thoughts.

Zach comes out of the adjoining bathroom, freshly showered, wearing a pair of white boxers. He walks over to his side of the bed and crawls under the covers next to me. He slips his arms around me and draws me close.

"Hey," he whispers.

"Hey," I say, hugging him back.

"I'm sorry. I've been so crazy the last couple of days," he says. "I know I've been obsessive. You know how I get."

"I do." We snuggle together, comfortably watching the movie. The bed is so cozy and warm.

Zach's ups and downs throughout the years have been numerous. But the good times far outweigh the bad. My thoughts travel to tenth grade in high school. I sprained my ankle in gym class, so the last month of school I hobbled around on crutches. Tabitha was supposed to help me carry my books and get my lunch in the cafeteria.

She did not. In fact, she avoided me all day. Zach stepped up. He carried my books to every class, got my lunch and brought it to the lunch table and then retrieved ice cream for dessert. He helped me with everything. It was the first time I saw him as more than just Zach, our childhood friend from down the road. So much more. He went out of his way if he cared for you. If you need him, he's there.

On the other hand though, Zach can explode at the slightest things. When we were seniors, one night the three of us were coming back from the movies, a car cut us off and Zach was outraged. He floored it and ran the car off the road. He wanted to use his baseball bat in the back seat from practice earlier that day to bash in the guy's windows. Tabitha and I talked him out of it. I remember how scared I felt in that moment. Zach was like a different person, full of rage, such a change from his usual personality. One other incident, when we were about ten years old, brought out the same fear in me. A girl had called Tabitha a name at school, I don't even remember what, and Zach slammed her against the brick wall in the recess area. Hard. She had a concussion. Luckily, she was okay, and Zach was suspended for a week and had to attend regular therapy sessions for his anger. The look in his eyes was so dark when he pushed her. Tabitha and I saw everything. He had the same look in the car that day. He's matured, though; I have never seen violence of that nature since, and those memories have faded over the years, but flickers of the unpredictability still exist. I've grown accustomed to his changing moods. Some years are worse than others.

He rubs my back, knowing all the places that feel the best to me.

"Did you like the flowers?" he asks, his breath hot on my neck.

I smile. "Yes, I do. Lilies are my favorite."

"Good." He continues to rub my back. "Do you really want to watch this movie?" he asks; his hands move down my back and cup my ass.

"Not really," I whisper back.

"You're not mad at me anymore?" he asks, kissing my neck.

"No, I can't stay mad at you," I say, returning his kiss. "I love you."

Later that night, I toss and turn in our bed. Zach snores in loud bursts beside me. I am never going to fall asleep if he keeps making so much noise. I pull the covers up tight to my neck and try to fall asleep, staring at the few streams of moonlight that pour through our bedroom shades and dance on our ceiling. Sleep eludes me so, a few minutes later, I give up, shove my feet into my pink memory foam slippers, grab my pink robe and slip out the bedroom door.

I pad downstairs and put a kettle on the stove to heat water for some tea. I open the glass cookie jar on the counter and take out a peanut butter cookie. I take a bite and glance at the clock. Three o'clock in the morning. I doubt I will fall asleep again, even though that is exactly what I need, sleep to clear my head. I'm probably up for the day.

I nibble on my cookie until the kettle whistles. Then I whisk it off the stove and pour the steaming water in with my Earl Grey and add a bit of milk and honey, then stroll over to the sofa. I sip my tea, considering turning on the TV, but decide against it. I rather enjoy the early morning silence. It's soothing, especially after the last few days.

Tabitha didn't call or text me all day, so unusual for her. We talk every day, so why did she ditch me today, especially after everything that happened? The weird interaction with Grant, and the breakfast with Anne exhausted me, even though I enjoyed the time I spent with her. Part of me still doesn't know what to think about Anne. So many questions swirl around her, mostly brought up by Tabitha. I need to listen to my own feelings. I feel that she is genuine. I like her.

At least everything is back to normal with Zach. The good times with him far outweigh his occasional erratic outbursts. I'm happy with that; I don't like to be at odds with him. I need him and I need him to be on my side, not Tabitha's.

I sit my cup on the coffee table and stretch out on the sofa. The soft chenille pillow cradles my face as I stare at the wall of windows in our kitchen and family room area, facing the backyard. The tan fabric blinds are all pulled down except two in the center. Moonlight streams in through the windows, making shadows on the gray hardwood floors.

My eyes close, willing a few more hours of sleep. The silence of the house calms me after the busyness of the day, but sleep eludes me, once again. I open my eyes.

A face stares at me through the uncovered window.

Then it is gone.

EIGHT

TABITHA

I park the car in the driveway and sit in the silence for a few moments. I look at my phone. Three missed calls from Talia and two texts. I chuckle; she misses me. I go away with someone else for the day and she's desperate to know everything. She doesn't care what I'm doing until it takes my attention away from her. She's been ditching me for years for other people and always acts so innocent. Let her wonder what I'm up to for a few hours, see how she likes it. I try to remember what age I became the "bad" twin and she the "good" twin. Probably around seven years old. Talia became friends with Jan Simples. Suddenly, she had a new best friend. They ate lunch together, played at recess together, even had a sleepover at our house. I have never seen a need for friends: Talia and I have each other; why would I want to spend time with someone else?

I wasn't good enough for Talia. Me! I hate how quickly she can drop me for a new friend. We are twins; we don't need other friends. One day at recess I held Jan Simples down on the grass and put red marker dots on her face. I called her Jan Pimples and soon all the kids were calling her that. Then Jan

Pimples didn't want to be around me or Talia. I had my sister back and I officially received the "bad" twin label.

I sigh. Shopping with Lucy and Ashley, Grant's sister, was tedious. I didn't even want to go, but Grant wanted me to since his insufferable sister was going too. I can't stand her dull talk about being a lawyer and her improv class. Grant has been acting cagey ever since he told me about the trouble at work; and now with Talia seeing a woman sneaking around the apartment, he is on another level of weird. His excuse of staying home today to check things didn't sit well with me. He's up to something, and I'll eventually find out what. I always do.

The apartment fiasco doesn't worry me much. I know who it was. Anne. I mentioned my theory to Grant, but he thinks I am being ridiculous. But something is off about Anne, something shady. Nothing about her moving here makes sense. I know Talia invited her out to lunch today: Zach mentioned it to me. Of course, she didn't invite me, another reason I went shopping today. I hate how Talia excludes me when she gets a new friend, like I don't even exist. She takes me for granted.

The question is what is Anne looking for in Little Beak? Did she find anything in the apartment that could hurt Grant, or us? Maybe Talia has the right idea. What's that old saying, keep your friends close, keep your enemies closer. I'm certain Anne is an enemy. Grant and Talia can't see that yet. I should ask Zach what he thinks about her. We usually agree on topics like this. He has the same gift as me, to see the darkness under what one presents to the world.

When I drive past Anne's house her curtains are open and she is talking to someone, not sure if it is a man or a woman, from my point of view. A shadowy form wearing what appears to be a baseball cap, I think, yet no car in the driveway and it is late. I need to investigate Anne more and find out exactly what she is up to and why she came to Little Beak.

I'll be the one watching her.

NINE

TALIA

A hand clamps over my mouth, suppressing my scream. It's my hand. I don't need to wake Zach. I know the face at the window.

Tabitha stands at my glass patio door in her blue silk pajamas. Her hair is up in a messy ponytail, and she wears no makeup. I open the door to let her inside.

"What are you doing here?" I ask. "You scared me to death!"

She walks in and sits on a stool at my kitchen island. She lifts the glass cookie jar and retrieves a peanut butter cookie. "I saw your light was on."

"How?"

She sighs. "I couldn't sleep, so I went outside."

"Checking the apartment?" I ask.

"I did and that's when I saw your kitchen light was on."

"Want some tea?"

"Sure."

"Did you have fun shopping with Lucy?"

"It was okay. She was so insistent for me to join her. Ashley came too."

I place her mug of tea on the counter. She takes a sip and sighs again.

"I was surprised to see Grant at home earlier."

"Yeah, he wanted to check for listening devices in the apartment. He had some other things to do that he didn't share with me."

"What is going on, Tabitha? Do you have any idea who that woman was?" I ask.

"It had to be Anne."

"I had breakfast with her today, uh, I guess it was yesterday."

Tabitha rolls her eyes. "And?"

"I don't know. I'm not sure what I think about her. I did find out something though."

"What?"

"We're considered the royalty of Little Beak." I laugh.

Tabitha's eyebrows arch. "Well, I knew that already. But, seriously, don't trust Anne. She's hiding something. I'm going to find out what it is."

"Did you notice if her lights were on, or hear any noise next door when you were watching?"

"No, nothing, but I'm going to find out why she moved here."

"And why Grant is acting so weird," I add.

"This reminds me of our Nancy Drew mysteries." Tabitha smiles. "I always figured them out before the end, way before you."

"Is this the mystery of the old clock or the hidden staircase?" I ask, laughing.

"The creepy writer next door." Tabitha grins, eating her cookie.

I laugh. "Get out your magnifying glass. We're on the case." I look at the clock. "Go home, maybe we can get a couple hours of sleep before we have to get ready for work."

. . .

The aroma of baking cupcakes fills the back room of Little Beak Sweets. I add another cup of flour into the bowl and flip on the stand mixer. I watch it swirl around for a bit and think about the decorating I plan for my finished batches. Another batch of vanilla and I'm finished with my morning baking, then I can move on to my favorite: decorating. Tabitha's the primary baker; it's always been her favorite. While I am always the first one at the shop, on Tuesdays, after our weekend, I have come in much earlier to bake. I pour the batter into the cupcake pans and put them into the commercial grade stove. A quick set of the timer and I get busy cleaning up the prep space. We have a couple cake orders, but those are for later in the week and Tabitha will take care of baking those orders.

I load the dishwasher and go over to my decorating area. My space. My large stainless-steel table sits against the exposed brick wall; sprinkles of every color line the wall along with boxes of decorating bags, various nozzles, cutouts, and some of my own personal decorating treats.

I add butter, powdered sugar, vanilla, and other ingredients into my red stand mixer. The hum of the machine fills the room. I love our workspace and what we do here, creating deliciousness and beauty for people. Pale pink walls, exposed brick on both sides of the room. Two large windows in the back of the room allow sunshine to fill it with warmth in the morning.

The mixer stops humming and I grab my decorating bag, adding the basketweave nozzle for the peanut butter frosting. I yawn. Waking up at 3 a.m. is catching up with me, despite the numerous cups of coffee I've had this morning. After the frosting is applied, I will start working on creating rose fondant flowers and tiny fondant autumn leaves for the cupcakes. So adorable.

"Good morning!" Claire's cheery voice calls as she walks in through the back door located between the two windows.

"Hey, Claire," I say. "How's it going?"

"Not bad," she replies, a carrier with two coffees in her hand. "Want one?"

"Yes, please." I accept the coffee, happy for the extra caffeine.

"Ooh, those look good," Claire says, eyeing the cupcakes. She snatches up a chocolate one and takes a huge bite. "Yum."

"Even without icing?" I laugh.

"Still the best," she says, wiping cupcake crumbs from her face. Her hair, a balayage bob, bounces as she nods. "Do anything fun this weekend?"

"I went out to breakfast yesterday with our new neighbor."

"Oh, is that the author?" Claire asks. "The moms were just talking about her at school. She has her own mystery going on here."

"Really, what did they say?"

"Well... I had to go into the school office to drop off my daughter's book report. It's a whole shoe box diorama and it's way too big to send with her on the bus, anyway Sue and Lydia were talking, you know Lydia is married to Chet, the realtor who listed the Edwards' house?"

"Yes."

"So, the Edwards had a decent offer on the house, but decided to rent it out for a year because she offered an exorbitant amount to do so. They figured they'd have no trouble selling the house later."

"That's so weird. Why would she offer so much?"

"That's why we were talking about it," Claire says. "I mean, there are so many places she could rent. Why insist on that particular house? Chet said she was so insistent on that specific house."

"Does Chet know why?"

"Anne told him she was working on a project. That's it." She sips her coffee. "You're right, it is weird. How did she seem to you?"

"Um... she was pleasant, but I didn't spend that much time with her, so my verdict is still out on her. She did say she is working on some new manuscripts. A trilogy. Maybe that's her project."

"Maybe that's it. Makes you wonder though. Like does she have some ulterior motive moving here? All of it is kind of strange."

"Definitely makes you wonder," I agree.

Tuesday night, I put a load of towels into the dryer and turn it on. I listen to it spin for a few minutes and then go out to the kitchen. A quick survey of the refrigerator has me selecting a string cheese. I'm peeling it open when a movement outside distracts me. I walk to the French doors.

A figure hunches over at the back of our yard, peering through the thick bushes to Anne's side. A figure wearing black leggings and a silver T-shirt.

Tabitha.

I open the door and creep up behind her. I move silently until I now stand inches from her.

"See anything?" I whisper.

She jumps and jams her head against the shrubbery; a branch jabs into her hair.

"What are you doing?" she hisses.

"What are *you* doing?" I reply.

Tabitha brushes the stick out of her hair. "Just keeping an eye on your best friend."

I shake my head. "So, you're snooping around my yard."

"If I lived here, I'd know what she was up to," she says, walking over to my patio table.

"She's not up to anything," I say. "You're paranoid."

"I'm doing what I've always done," she replies. "Taking care of you, dear sister."

"I can take care of myself."

Tabitha rolls her eyes.

TEN

TALIA

Wednesday morning is busy, which is nice because time passes quickly. I glance at the clock. Tabitha will be in soon. I ring up a customer's order. One dozen cupcakes, six vanilla confetti and six chocolate salted caramel, all nestled in a pink box. I pause for a moment before closing the box, admiring their frosted beauty, and smile at how something as simple as a cupcake can brighten someone's day.

"Thank you!" I say, handing the pink box to the lady. "Have a great day!"

The woman murmurs a goodbye, takes the box and walks out, the door jingling her exit. I rearrange the cupcake case, making sure everything is presented equally. Then wipe the counter until it shines; I am a bit of a clean freak.

Our shop is adorable; maybe I'm prejudiced, but I don't see how anyone wouldn't love this space. Pink and white striped walls, a large glass display showing off our cakes and cupcakes. A charming, large clock, shaped like a cupcake, in pink and white, hangs above the customer counter. A few antique white round tables, with matching chairs, pink and white striped cushions to make a comfortable seat. Checkered black and white tile floor stretching across the entire store. A cooler, also housed in antique white wood, at the side filled with Fiji Water, iced coffee, and various juice drinks.

The door jingles again. A tall, handsome, middle-aged man with a well-trimmed dark beard and a few graying hairs at his temples walks inside.

"Hi, Dan," I say. I grab a large pink box from the counter behind me. "Your order is ready. Since you prepaid, you're all set."

"Thanks, Talia." Dan smiles. He runs the local bookstore, next door to us, only opened for about a year, but it has quickly become a popular spot. "We're having book club today and everyone loves your cupcakes."

"Oh, thanks so much," I say. "We always love to hear that!"

Dan waves goodbye, and my cell phone rings. Tabitha.

"Hey," I answer.

"I need you to come over to my house," she says. "Now."

"What?"

"Have Claire watch the shop. Come over now," she demands and then hangs up.

What is going on with her now? Worry filters through me. I put my phone in my jeans pocket and call for Claire. She is in the back stocking supplies. I tell her I have to go help Tabitha with something and I'll be back in a couple hours.

I race out to my car and back out of the parking spot. Grabbing my sunglasses off the dashboard and putting them on, I tear out of the parking lot and head toward Tabitha's house, my tires spinning and stones flying up, hitting the bumper. Something must have happened with Grant. Or what if that woman came back to Tabitha's house and tried to break in? I gasp and press on the gas.

I'm speeding and hope I don't pass any cops on the five-minute drive to her house. I glance in my rearview mirror then slam on the brakes, almost running a stop sign. I better slow down; I don't need to get into an accident.

I look both ways at the stop sign and proceed to her house at a reasonable speed. I go up her driveway, park, and run into the house. She sits on her expansive deep-seated gray sofa in her family room. The fireplace is going, warming the space. A daytime talk show playing on the huge flat-screen TV over the gas fireplace. Tears streak her face, her nose bright red from rubbing it, likely a casualty of the pile of used tissues lying beside her on the sofa.

"Tabitha." I walk in and sit down beside her. She holds the daisy barrette in her hand.

"I found the owner of this barrette," she snaps. "I know exactly who was in the apartment on Saturday night."

"What, who?"

"Kim Metlock, the crunch queen."

"Oh..."

Kim is a fitness model who goes to our gym. She's known as the crunch queen, her self-given title because of how many crunches she does during a workout, even has a poster at the gym that updates how many crunches she does on that particular day. A gym legend. Every woman wants to look like her and every straight guy fantasizes about her. She was in *Shape* magazine last year. She's gorgeous.

"Why would she be there?"

Tabitha blows her nose again. "I'll give you one guess."

I shake my head. "I have no idea."

"Grant is having an affair with her!" Tabitha yells, and her voice cracks.

"Are you serious?" I ask. "Are you sure?"

"Yes, I'm sure!"

"How did you find out?"

"Remember Saturday when we were working later to fill that big cupcake order?"

"Yeah, we got home around four. And we were rushing because you had to get ready for the charity dinner."

"Well, Grant was home alone, because Cole was visiting at a friend's house. I picked him up on the way home from work. Kim came over to see Grant. Apparently, they have been seeing each other for a few months, but usually at hotels in the city. I guess this was the first time in the apartment."

"Oh..." I say, touching her shoulder. I hate to see my sister in such pain. I know she must be dying inside. She brushes my hand off.

"So, Kim comes back to the apartment Saturday night because she left her cell phone there when her and Grant were having *sex* earlier in the day."

"Really?" I shake my head.

"Yes, she texted him before we left for the charity dinner, and he left the door unlocked for her." Tabitha sighs.

"Wow," I say. This is crazy.

"And you know how you mentioned how weird it was that Grant took Monday off work? That jog he was taking was over to Kim's apartment to break it off with her."

"Wow," I repeat, for lack of a better word to all her news. "How did you know it was her barrette?"

"She was on the elliptical next to me at the gym this morning. She had an identical barrette on, so I confronted her." Tabitha gives a rueful laugh. "She just crumbled, crying and apologizing to me. I didn't shed a tear."

"Oh, Tabitha." I soften my voice. "That must have been so hard for you."

Tears spring to her eyes. "It was," she says in a small voice. She hugs me. "How could he cheat on me? How am I going to face him tonight? He's ruined everything. Why is he so stupid!"

"You'll figure it out," I console her. "Let Cole sleep over at our house tonight so you two can talk."

"Thank you." Tabitha grabs a handful of tissues from the box sitting on the end table and wipes her tears away. "I'm going to kill Grant."

"Well, not really?" I state, a question in my voice. Given her mindset now, I'm not sure.

"No, Talia, not really, but it's going to be bad."

"I know." I squeeze her again. Tears fall from my eyes too.

"I won't be seeing Kim again, at least at the gym."

"Why, what did you do?"

"She said she's switching gyms. She doesn't want to see Grant or me ever again."

"I imagine not," I reply, hugging my sister.

ELEVEN

TABITHA

I grab another tissue and blow my nose. Tears choke me and I sit still, trying to calm my body, still spasming. I held it together somewhat while Talia was here but now, the tears will not stop. My husband is betraying me, and he doesn't seem to care one bit. And at our own home!

How can Grant do this? Sleeping with Kim? He promised this would never happen again. My stomach churns thinking about the first time. Or at least the first time I knew of. Seven years ago, he had an affair with a woman at work. I was pregnant with Cole and devastated. I never told anyone, not even Talia, I was so embarrassed. And I believed his promise that it would never happen again. He kept that promise, or so I thought, for years: We had Cole, we redecorated our beautiful home. We were happy living a good life and now, this. Was he lying the entire time?

My body calms and I sit on the sofa, unmoving. I'll never leave him, but I will not accept him cheating on me. He must understand this is absolutely the last time or he will never be with me again. The one thing that has never soured in our marriage is our sex life. He will never give up what we have—he just wants all the extras, too.

Grant and I married when I was twenty-one and he was twenty-four years old. I was clueless about the prenup agreement his parents had me sign, and my parents were just as clueless about it. At the time, it didn't matter, I was so in love with Grant, still am, and I didn't care how much money we had, or didn't have.

With the prenup, if we divorced, I'd get one million dollars. That's it, no splitting our assets, the house, investments, nothing. A flat million dollars. A tidy sum for a twenty-something with no children. But now, with a child and living a particular lifestyle, one million wouldn't go very far. I could never stay in this house and the bakery does well, but if I had to survive on the income, I'd be moving back upstate.

We will work things out though, like always. My thoughts drift back to sophomore year of college when I met Grant for the first time. I was on a school sponsored trip with a group from college to sightsee in NYC. Broadway show, Times Square, Rockefeller Center, all the usual tourist traps. We were standing outside The New York Stock Exchange taking pictures and drinking strawberry smoothies when this unbelievably gorgeous guy came up to me and said, "Hi, I'm Grant. What's your name?" No games, no shyness, just introduced himself with complete confidence. I was in love.

He wore a well-tailored suit, had slicked back, thick blond hair and stunning ocean blue eyes. This was no college boy. This was a man.

He was interning on Wall Street and only had a few minutes to talk, but he got my cell number and called me that night. I never met anyone like him, and his Manhattan world fascinated me. He lived on Madison Avenue with his parents, and it was a world away from my small-town home upstate.

The sexual chemistry sparked immediately. We craved each

other day and night, we couldn't get enough. The attraction and love between us seemed unreal, like a dream, to me, certainly nothing I experienced with any other boyfriends. When he got a permanent job position, he proposed, and our life evolved to what it is today.

Talia can't possibly understand my relationship with Grant. Her marriage to Zach is different because we've known him almost all our lives. She knew what she was getting into with him and knew how to manage their life, which she does well. I know Zach isn't easy to live with, but Talia does it with ease. Grant is constantly throwing me curveballs in our marriage, some good, some terrible. Once I think I understand him and where we are going as a couple, there's another turn I did not expect.

I glance up to the clock on the fireplace mantle. My gaze stops at the family photograph in an embossed silver frame next to the clock. Grant, Cole and me, all dressed in white, smiling, on the beach in front of Grant's family beach home in the Hamptons. Why didn't Grant appreciate us, appreciate his family, respect his wife and child? Why would he bring his infidelity into our lives? I sigh and look away from the photo. Cole will be home soon and so will Grant. I struggle to my feet and go upstairs to clean myself up and handle this situation. Why do I feel so alone in every relationship I have?

Two days later, I open the door to Cole's classroom at school, on my usual Friday volunteer morning, but today is special. The classroom fizzes with excitement, including two first grade girls who are dancing in the back of the room. I smile at them, twirling in frilly skirts and having the time of their life. I wish I still felt that kind of joy. I go to the crescent-shaped table at the side and place my Tupperware dish, housing fresh baked mini apple pies, on top of it. Cole runs over to me and gives me a hug.

"Mommy!" he exclaims. "Are you here for reader's theater?"

"Yes, and I brought those little apple pies we made last night."

His eyes widen. "Oh, yum." Then he darts back to his group sitting on carpet squares at the front of the room rehearsing their play, or reader's theater, as they called it. The SMART board behind where they sit is playing soothing music as the first graders read their lines together.

Last night we baked mini apple pies and enjoyed a quiet evening, quite a difference from the night prior when Cole slept over at Talia's house. Grant and I had an enormous argument about him and Kim and the promises he had made to me, and broken, again. He was apologetic and promised me things would be different this time, same as he had in the past. Did I believe him? I'm not sure, but I let out my full rage at him and made it clear the decisions he chooses impact our entire family, not just him. I felt like he listened to me, at least, and being heard is the first step. I want to work on our relationship; I don't want to break up the life we created. I hope he will make a change for all of us to grow and continue as a family. For now, things are mending, and I'm hopeful they will continue to improve.

Today I look forward to seeing Cole's reader theater. His teacher, Mrs. Kramer, told us it was to be a presentation about Johnny Appleseed in the Tall Tales section of the curriculum, and she would appreciate apple-based snacks. So far, the crescent-shaped table consists of apple juice, apple slices, apple cookies, applesauce, and my mini apple pies.

"Hey, Tabitha." I turn to see Claire walk inside the room, carrying a grocery bag. She sits it on the table.

"Hi, Claire," I say. Her daughter is in Cole's class. "What did you bring?"

She smirks. "Apple-flavored lollipops. Not the healthiest snack, but that's what my daughter insisted on bringing."

I laugh. "I'm sure they'll be a big hit."

Mrs. Kramer motions to the parents to find a seat in the back of the classroom. Claire and I sit next to each other on the first-grade-size blue plastic chairs. Other parents follow suit, and we settle in to watch the show.

"I saw your new neighbor at the grocery store," Claire remarks. "Anne? Talia and I were talking about her the other day."

"Really? What were you talking about?" I ask, curious.

"Oh, she didn't tell you? I was talking to Lydia, and you know she's married to Chet, the realtor that listed the Edwards' house."

"Yes." I nod.

"They had offers on the house, but Anne offered an enormous sum to rent it for one year. An offer they couldn't refuse."

"I knew that house was listed for sale, not rent. Do you know why she wanted to rent it so badly?"

"No, I don't. I'm surprised Talia didn't tell you about it."

"OK, everyone, Mrs. Kramer's first grade class presents... Johnny Appleseed!" the teacher exclaims.

We get quiet and watch our children perform their reader's theater. One question, or two, run through my mind. Why didn't Talia tell me about it? What other secrets does Talia keep from me? First my husband, now Talia; is everyone betraying me?

TWELVE

TALIA

The dishwasher, filled to capacity, runs loudly in the kitchen. I think we may soon need a new one. Tonight is leftover spaghetti for dinner. I have eaten, but Zach still isn't home from work, so his serving still sits in the refrigerator.

I have grabbed my cell phone to call him when I hear the garage door open. A few minutes later, he walks inside. He comes over to me, a wide smile on his face, and gives me a long hug.

I laugh, enjoying his embrace. "Oh, you should come home like this every night."

He kisses me, so happy. "My new promotion is official. This afternoon I was thinking how much this extra income is going to do for us, for our family."

Tears well in my eyes. "Our family."

Zach touches my face, trailing down my cheekbone. "I love you, Talia. I really want to have a baby with you. Now we don't have to worry about the cost of IVF. It's something we can do. I know we've been hesitating, but I think we should go for it."

"Really?" I say, excitement coloring my voice. I hug him

tight. This is the first time he has seemed as excited as me about starting a family.

"Something else, too." He reaches into the pocket of his dress pants and pulls out a small white box with a red ribbon tied around it. He hands it to me.

"Ooh... what's this?" I ask, pulling the ribbon off.

"Remember that ruby ring I got you when we were dating, that got lost when we moved here?"

"Yeah," I say. Even years later, the loss of that ring still stings. I lost weight and the ring was loose and needed to be resized. I had it in a small jewelry box, along with some favorite earrings, and other baubles. We never found it.

"Well, I saw this at a jewelry store, and it reminded me of that ring, but so much more," he says.

I open the box and inside is the most beautiful red ruby ring on a polished gold band and a sparkling diamond on either side of it. Stunning.

"Oh, Zach, I love it!" I exclaim, quickly putting it on my finger to admire.

"When I saw this, it made me think of the family we are starting," he says. "You are the ruby, the heart of the family, and the diamonds on either side are me and our baby we will have one day."

Tears spill from my eyes. I can't love him more than I love him in this moment. Love fills my heart and my entire body for this man. I wrap my arms around him and hold him close to me. This is the Zach I love with all my heart. This is the Zach who loves me.

Whole Foods buzzes with busy shoppers filling their baskets with all the contents on their weekly grocery lists. Plump peaches, organic carrots, green leafy kale, strawberry jam, and fresh baked bread, are piled high in carts around me. The line at the meat counter is long and tedious, mostly due to the older woman in front of me in line telling me about her tendonitis and aching back. Then another ten minutes with her extremely specific instructions for her meat order. I breathe a sigh of relief when she hobbles away with her cart.

I pause by the bakery and inhale the delicious aroma, picking up two loaves of French bread. My grocery cart is getting quite full in preparation for our dinner party tonight. I'm making roast beef, garlic green beans, mashed potatoes with gravy, and a chocolate raspberry filled cake for dessert, with chocolate icing. The president of the bank Zach works for, and his wife, are coming over this evening. The day Zach brought home the ruby ring for me, he also brought good news to celebrate. He is being promoted to Regional Vice President and now will be working in Manhattan. Increased salary and responsibility also means increased socializing, so Zach wants to start off on the right foot in his new position, and I'm happy to help him make a smooth transition. I pause for a moment to admire the ruby and diamond ring Zach gave me a few nights ago, my heart swelling with love for him and excitement for our future, even given his recent temperament.

Fresh flowers are next on my list. I peruse the selection and settle on a lovely assortment of various roses, red, pink, yellow, peach; I love the burst of color. I stare at the flower display, my thoughts drifting over the last few days. Tabitha confronted Grant with his infidelity. He promised everything was over with Kim and begged her to give him another chance, which she did. I wasn't surprised: Grant is her soft spot. I think she will forgive him for almost anything, at least once. I wonder if I'd be as forgiving with Zach in that same situation.

Sometimes I wonder if I really know Zach. His behavior is all over the map. Those lovely lilies he got me to say he was sorry turned into another argument. He had a fit because after a few days they were dying, saying I didn't take care of them.

News flash, fresh flowers die quickly. But then, he surprises me with this beautiful ring and the sentiment behind it is even more beautiful. He confuses me.

Another person pops into my mind. I haven't thought of her since all this Tabitha and Grant drama started swirling around. Anne. We were wrong about her. All those suspicions were silly, figments of our overactive imaginations. Sometime soon I'll invite Anne to go shopping, really give her a chance. Maybe we'll become good friends.

But now, I have a dinner to make. I grab another bouquet of flowers, pink and purple lilies, my favorite flower, with delicate baby's breath, and put them in my cart, quickly heading to the checkout counter.

Candlelight flickers on our well-set dining table. Silver linen tablecloth, white bone china, matching silver cloth napkins, elegant etched wine glasses. Roses placed in the center of the table. Perfect.

Zach walks in from the kitchen carrying two glasses of merlot. He hands me one and winks. "Everything looks great. Need help with anything?"

"No, I think we're good," I say, sipping the wine.

Zach adjusts the collar on his pinstriped green dress shirt and sits his wine glass on the table. He leans down to kiss me. "You look amazing. New dress?"

"Yes." I smile, smoothing the sides of my pale, rose-colored sheath dress. "Thank you."

"I'm so excited about this promotion, Talia," he says. "This will be so great for us."

"And I'm excited for you. You've worked hard, you deserve it."

"The only downside is that I'll be away from home more. Longer commute, but the money more than makes up for it."

I nod. "Oh, yes it does. Maybe a beach house in our future?"

"Maybe." He smiles. "That would be amazing."

I walk out to the kitchen to retrieve the breadbasket and place it on the table and straighten two forks. I look at him and smile. "I'm so proud of you."

He kisses me again. "Thanks for doing all of this. Jim and Lindsay will love it."

"I hope so," I reply as our doorbell rings. We go to greet our guests.

Dinner turns out delicious and the company pleasant, our conversation takes many interesting directions and by dessert we are stuffed, but still manage some cake, of course.

"Talia, I must ask you something," Lindsay says, touching her fresh-from-the-salon blowout hair. "Zach told Jim that Anne Graveley, the author, lives next door to you."

I nod. "Yes, she moved in a few weeks ago."

"I love her novels. I've read all of them." Lindsay smiles. "I'm a bit embarrassed to admit I brought her newest one with me tonight. Do you think she'd sign it for me?"

"She probably would. Let me text her and ask," I say, getting up to retrieve my phone.

> Hey, Anne. We have some guests over and one is a huge fan of your books. Would you mind signing a book she brought along?

Three dots appear immediately.

> Sure, I'll be over in ten minutes.

> Thanks, Anne!

I plug my phone back in the charger on the kitchen counter and go back to the dining room.

"Good news, Lindsay, she'll be over soon," I announce.

"Yes!" Lindsay jumps up. "I'll go get my book!"

"Well, you made her night," Jim says, laughing. "That's all she talked about on the way here."

"I read one of Anne's books," Zach says. "It was good. I enjoyed it."

"I didn't know that," I reply. "I'll have to check them out. I've been meaning to, but everything has been so busy lately."

A few minutes later, Lindsay, along with Anne, comes back into the house. Anne's dressed in jeans, black sweater, and cute short black suede boots. Her thick, normally curly hair is straightened, and dark, well-applied makeup highlights her face. Long, dangly silver earrings hang from her ears.

"You look great, Anne," I compliment her. "Do you have a date tonight?"

"Thanks, I'm meeting some friends later for drinks," Anne replies. "I can't stay long."

Lindsay already introduced Anne to her husband, Jim, and I need to follow suit.

"Anne, this is my husband, Zach," I say, smiling.

Zach grins and extends his hand, which Anne coolly accepts. "Zach," she says in a crisp tone, far less friendly than she greeted Lindsay or Jim.

"Nice to meet you, Anne," he replies, a warm smile on his handsome face.

Anne only smiles and nods, quickly pulling her hand from his. Why does she seem so uncomfortable? She turns back to Lindsay and speaks in a friendly tone to her. Whatever awkwardness existed dissolves and I wonder if I imagined it in the first place.

Lindsay hands her the book. "Could you make it out to Lindsay, with an a," she says. "I love your writing. I never know where the story is going, always such a shock at the end."

"Thank you, Lindsay," Anne says, signing the book.

"What are you working on now?" Lindsay asks, her brown eyes full of excitement.

"A trilogy," replies Anne. "I got some good news today. My first book has been optioned for a movie. We're going out tonight to celebrate."

"That's awesome!" I exclaim.

"Congratulations!" Zach and Jim chime in.

"Oh, my goodness, I can't wait to see it! Congratulations, Anne!" Lindsay cheers. "I can't believe I'm one of the first people to hear about the movie. So exciting!"

"Want some wine, Anne?" I ask. "No, Zach, go get champagne, it's in the basement."

"No, don't bother." Anne shakes her head. "I appreciate the sentiment, but I do have to leave." She turns to Lindsay. "I'm glad I was here to sign your book. I'm so glad you enjoy my stories; I certainly enjoy writing them."

They say goodbyes and Anne leaves to meet her friends. I pour another glass of wine and Lindsay does the same. The guys walk out on the patio so Jim can smoke.

Lindsay clutches her book. "She is one of my favorite authors. This one"—she holds up the book—"took place in upstate New York. The twist at the end with the kids blew me away. I won't go into too much detail since you haven't read it yet."

I sip my wine. "I'll download them tonight on my Kindle. Your high praise really piqued my interest."

Tabitha and I walk into Bear Bear, an adorable children's clothing shop on Main Street in Little Beak. The store sells clothing for infants up to teen sized, ranging from so cute to so cool. We are looking for the so cool category. Cole informed Tabitha he didn't want anything cutesy. He is six years old.

"Let's go upstairs," she suggests as we browse the first floor. "Most of the boys' clothes are up there. Cole needs some long-sleeve pullovers and jeans."

I nod, lingering at the infant onesies and sweet sleepers in an array of pale colors. Will I be buying some of these in the future? I glance at my ruby ring. Maybe.

We go upstairs and browse the boys' clothing. Tabitha selects a dark green pullover and a creamy yellow one. She also puts a couple athletic-style sweatshirts and two pairs of jeans into her basket.

Tabitha holds up another with little skulls on it. "Cole would like this one."

I smile. "Sure would, perfect for under his Halloween costume."

Tabitha puts the shirt down. "I don't know how I'm going to do this."

"What?" I ask, moving closer to her. Tabitha's behavior worries me. I know she has internalized the overwhelming hurt she must feel from Grant's infidelity. I fear when she does let out those feelings it will be explosive. I want to help her in any way I can.

She whispers in my ear: "I think I'm going to hire a private investigator."

My eyes widen. "You are? To follow Grant?"

She nods. "I think so."

"How do you even find a private investigator?" I wonder out loud.

"You can find anything on the Internet," she snaps. "Seriously, Talia, it's like you live in a bubble."

"Sure, well do you think it's a good idea?"

"I haven't decided yet. Maybe I'll just follow them around?" she says, picking up the shirt again.

"Them?"

"Grant and Anne," she snaps again.

"Oh," I say.

I do *not* think that is a good idea.

THIRTEEN

TALIA

The four of us enter the Wall Street Grill and are graciously shown our table close to the bar. Warm glowing candles flicker on every table and wine glasses stand tall awaiting their task. The glass ceiling above our table reveals a million white twinkling lights of the city, and a few bright stars, and bursts of lush greenery draped high on the walls amidst white lights. Long pendant lights hang at the bar, already crowded with patrons eager to get their dinner chardonnay or cabernet. I was going for a French Manhattan tonight.

We get settled, order our drinks, and peruse the menu. Grant and Zach met us here after work. Cole is staying with Grant's parents for the weekend, so we decided to celebrate Zach's promotion. It has been months since we've gone out to dinner in the city, and I'm happy we decided to come.

Our drinks arrive and our appetizer, duck spring rolls, and everyone gives their orders to the server. We all order steaks, except Tabitha: She orders the salmon. The restaurant buzzes with happy diners; we were lucky to get a reservation.

"I had lunch here a couple weeks ago," Grant says. "The food is great."

"Good to know," replies Zach. "I hate overcooked or under-cooked steak."

Grant agrees and I tune out their discussion on how a steak should be cooked. Not that I don't appreciate a well-cooked steak. I have other things on my mind. While it's fun to be out to dinner together, it is a bit weird too. Everyone sitting at this table knows Grant cheated on, or is still cheating on, Tabitha. If I were in her shoes, going out to dinner together would be the last thing I'd want to do, and this is her idea, but who knows? We all play a part and make sacrifices doing things we otherwise wouldn't necessarily choose to do.

Tabitha nudges my arm and motions over to the bar. Anne stands there in a stylish mid-length black dress and dressy black sandals, her hair up in a loose twist, long tendrils framing her face. She talks amicably to the bartender, a man in his mid-twenties with shaggy surfer-like blond hair and a disarming grin.

Anne.

"Is she following us?" Tabitha whispers to me.

"I doubt it. Was she on the train?" I ask.

"I didn't see her, but she must have been."

"Maybe she was here before us. She used to live in Manhattan, so I'm sure she has plenty of friends in the city," I suggest. "Who knows, maybe family."

"If she had family in the city, why would she be living in Little Beak?"

"Not everyone lives next door to their siblings. In fact, most don't," I retort.

Grant and Zach are now staring at us. We point to the bar.

"Is that the new neighbor?" Grant asks.

Zach nods. "Yeah, Anne."

A tall, bearded man, about mid-forties, approaches the bar and signals to the bartender for a drink. Anne looks at him and says something. He glances at her, recognition registering in his face, and he smiles at her.

"Is that Dan from the bookstore?" Zach asks.

"It is," says Tabitha. We all stare at them.

Our food arrives. The flurry of several servers bringing our food blocks the view of the bar for a few moments. Now all our delicious food sits on the table in front of us ready to enjoy, but Anne is gone. So is the blond bartender.

Dan walks toward us.

"Hi, Dan!" Grant greets, always the gregarious one.

Dan holds a glass of red wine. "Hello, everyone. Seems like the residents of Little Beak are all in Manhattan tonight."

"Are you here with Anne?" Tabitha asks, cutting to the chase. "We saw you two at the bar."

"No, I was surprised to see her. I'm meeting a friend here," he says, and he looks at the door when it opens and an attractive brunette walks in. "Oh, there she is. Have a good evening."

Dan leaves to join his friend. We look at each other.

"That was kind of weird," Tabitha says.

"Not really." Grant shakes his head. "He was just meeting a date here."

"I guess you would know about meeting dates," Tabitha snarls.

Grant stares at her. "Really?"

"She has a point," Zach mutters. He and Grant glare at one another for a moment, then each start cutting their steaks.

"Where did Anne go?" I ask. "Did she leave or is she still here?"

Probably watching us.

"That bartender is gone too, probably done with his shift for the night," Grant says, cutting into his steak. "Maybe she went somewhere with him. They seemed to hit it off."

I slowly cut my steak, putting a small piece into my mouth. Juicy, soft, and tender, everything you want in a steak. I keep my gaze focused on the bar and its surroundings. The blond bartender doesn't reappear.

Neither does Anne.

"So, what do you think about last night?" Tabitha asks. We are at Little Beak Sweets; she puts in another batch of lemon cupcakes, and I add sprinkles to the double chocolate cupcakes at my workstation. A half-eaten cupcake sits by my morning coffee. I can't resist chocolate. And double chocolate? Not a chance.

"I think it's strange that Anne just disappeared. Maybe she went with that bartender like Grant said, but still strange. Do you think she saw us? Dan did."

"I agree. And I would imagine she saw us, but why not come over to say hi?" Tabitha replies. "Do you know what I noticed last night?"

"What?" I continue sprinkling the confetti-style decoration atop the frosting.

"Dan is a good-looking guy," says Tabitha.

"Yeah, right? I never noticed that before either. Maybe because it was a different environment."

"I guess," replies Tabitha. "Still strange that he and Anne were there at the same time as us."

"Coincidences happen. I think that's all it was. I did have a nice time. The food was great," I say.

"I did too, surprising given the circumstances."

"Things seemed a little rough with you and Grant," I remark.

"They are. It's going to take time for us to work through everything."

Grant and Cole are the only ones who have Tabitha's true loyalty. Grant's the only one she will forgive for such a betrayal. I often wonder why she doesn't extend the same consideration to me when I never did anything remotely as hurtful as Grant. I can get a new friend I enjoy spending time with, and she flips out. She always says we are twins and don't need other friends, but I don't see the harm in having friends. I wouldn't be upset if she had a new friend, but she never does, possibly because of her abrasive personality.

"You know what I was thinking?" she asks, pulling me out of my thoughts. "We should add pies to our menu. Mini pies. Apple, cherry, chocolate, and maybe key lime pie."

"Pie," I repeat. "Maybe."

Anne and I know when to hit the café and avoid crowds. She spotted me puttering around the yard earlier and asked if I'd like to join her for an early lunch, or late breakfast—the café serves both all day. Monday is usually my catch-up around the house day, or relax day.

We both put in an order for Palm Beach shrimp salad and mimosas. Anne and I are very similar in some ways.

"Cheers," she says, clinking our glasses.

"I'm so glad you invited me to lunch," I say, spearing a piece of lettuce and shrimp. "We saw you at the Wall Street Grill on Friday night."

Anne looks at me. "Oh, I was meeting a friend for drinks. You should have said hello."

"We were eating dinner and just saw you for a few minutes at the bar."

Anne nods.

Our talks usually are about broad subjects, movies, books, the town, sometimes about my family. I notice she never brings up her family or relationships, which I find a bit odd.

"So, do you have any brothers or sisters?" I ask.

Anne shakes her head. "No. My mother died when I was young. I never knew my birth father."

"Oh, I'm so sorry," I quickly say. I feel like a jerk now. There's a reason she doesn't speak about her family.

"Yeah, life wasn't easy for me when I was younger." She pauses. "I was in foster care and sometimes it got rough."

"I'm sure it did. I'm sorry I brought it up. We can talk about something else," I reply.

"But then I met my adoptive parents, Charles and Millie, and they were wonderful people. Very good to me," Anne says, a loving look in her eye. "I got lucky."

"Oh, I'm so glad," I reply.

"They passed away a couple years ago, but I will always be thankful for the love and kindness they gave me," Anne sighs. "This is some heavy lunch talk."

"Sure is, hey let's get dessert and we'll talk about something lighter." I pick up the dessert menu. "Crème brûlée or key lime pie?"

"How about one of each and we share?"

"Yes!" I exclaim, smiling at her.

The dessert arrives in record time, half of each on two plates, and we enjoy their sweetness. The conversation moves on to other topics and I hope Anne doesn't mind my earlier blunder in bringing up her childhood.

FOURTEEN

TALIA

A week or so after our dinner at the Wall Street Grill, I find myself in Manhattan once again. The city pulsates with energy and noise, a departure from my normal daily routine in Little Beak. I inhale the fresh aroma from a nearby popcorn vendor and take a moment to enjoy the masses of people moving around me, all consumed with their own personal agenda and destinations. The bright lights, endless choices of restaurants and shopping and the magnetic, energetic vibe vibrating through the city draws me in. Manhattan, always the drama queen, and me, always anxious to watch her show.

I pause for a moment, the taxis honking their horns, tourists scurrying around me, some stopping at a nearby display of knock-off Louis Vuitton purses, and several people beside me speaking Chinese, barely registering in my mind as I stand staring at a tall building on East 60th Street. This might be the appointment that changes my life. Our life.

Zach is already somewhere inside, sitting in a waiting room; he texted me a few moments ago. In a few minutes, I'll be inside talking to an IVF doctor to see if having a baby is a possibility for us. While I'm not one hundred percent sure this is the route for us to take, I want to explore the option more. We want a baby more than anything, me more so than Zach, and it only makes sense to get all the details on the process.

Nerves trickle through me. I want this, but I'm hesitant too; at a bare minimum, getting all the information we can gather and deciding on that information is the best place to start.

I walk inside the door and make my way to the elevator inside the plush office building. As the elevator makes its way to the appropriate floor, my anticipation grows, a million questions forming in my mind. Luckily, I've written most of those questions down since they've been plaguing me from when I made this appointment. Making lists is a way to calm my nerves. If I write something out, it's out of my head and on paper. I can stop running it repeatedly in my mind.

The elevator rings my arrival and I'm relieved to see Zach sitting on a large white sofa to the left of the reception area. He's paging through an issue of a golfing magazine. I walk over to him, after checking in, and sink beside him. He puts his hand over mine, sensing my nervousness.

A few minutes pass and then a nurse calls us back. A few more minutes and we are sitting in Dr. Labinsky's large, sunny, modern-style office discussing our medical histories, results of tests we've completed, and what more testing is needed to prepare the best plan for our fertility care. I appreciate her caring, open demeanor and the discussion is a good first step in seeing if this is something we want to explore. This is an important decision we are making and not one to jump into, but rather with great consideration.

Zach needs to leave early. He has a meeting at the bank that can't be missed, so I stay a bit longer and Dr. Labinsky talks about the emotional toll IVF takes on a couple, both as a couple and as individuals. This is a concern for me, more about Zach than myself. Is this process something he could handle? He's the more emotional one, whereas I'm more the steady, logical one. I don't have the same ups and downs that he does. He already has the pressure of his new job, so would adding this to his plate be too much for him? Even though it would be more of a physical stress on me than him.

An hour later, loaded with a wealth of information, brochures, and future test appointments, I enter the elevator once more. A few floors down, it stops, allowing a beautiful woman to step inside. She holds a lovely tan Gucci purse and a large brochure, *Pregnancy and You*. A beautiful, familiar woman.

Kim Metlock.

She turns and looks directly at me. Surprise covers her face. She opens her purse and shoves the brochure inside.

"Tabi..." she begins, then stops herself. "Oh, hi, Talia."

"Hi, Kim," I say. "Are you...?"

The elevator stops again, allowing more people to enter. Kim ignores my question and runs out of the elevator.

FIFTEEN
TALIA

Later in the day I walk over to Tabitha's house and spring the news on her, or at least what I observed in the city. "She's pregnant?" Tabitha yells when I tell her, jumping out of the lush, muted silver lounge chair. She paces up and down the length of their newly installed heated pool. It's the first week of October, but we swim in bliss most of the afternoon. At least they'll get a couple weeks to use it before closing it for the winter months.

"I don't know for sure, but why else would she have a *Pregnancy and You* brochure?"

"So, she was coming from the gynecologist?"

"I guess so, there's all kinds of doctors in that building," I reply.

"But you aren't sure there's a gynecologist on that floor?" Tabitha asks.

"No, I didn't check, but where else would she get that brochure? And she tried to hide it from me by shoving it inside her purse."

Tabitha sighs. "To hell with all of this! I shouldn't have to deal with any of it. What was Grant thinking? All I should be doing today is lying by my new pool drinking a mai tai. Now I have to think about freaking Kim Metlock and a freaking baby! Do you think it's Grant's?"

I remain silent. I don't know what to say.

Tabitha puts on a white robe and sits on the end of my lounge chair. She arches her eyebrows. "She's been texting him. A lot. He showed me."

"What's she saying?"

"She loves him. She wants to see him, he's so important to her. She can't stop thinking about him, that kind of shit; she's so pathetic. He deletes all of them."

I snort. "That's what he tells you."

She glares at me. "He's not lying to me. He promised he'd never cheat on me again."

"I hope that's true. I really do, Tabitha. You and Grant were so happy before all of this, at least you seemed to be."

"We were. We are." Tabitha shakes her head. "It happened, but it's over now. He knows he was wrong."

"But would he have broken it off if I hadn't seen her going into the apartment that night?"

"I don't know," Tabitha says. "But she can't be pregnant."

"Maybe it's not his," I suggest.

"You always were a positive thinker, Talia." She smirks. "But if she is pregnant, I'm sure it is."

"We'll find out soon," I say.

I stand up and sit at the pool's edge, dangling my legs in the warm water. I slide down, allowing it to envelop me, and swim across its length. Long fingers of sunshine heat my upturned face, and I drink in the heat. I'm sure we won't have many more days like this left before autumn creeps in. Tabitha's outdoor oasis has turned out beautifully. The kidney-shaped pool curves into a rock waterfall in the rear and moves into a hot tub toward the front of the pool. Jets of water spurt by the side of the water-fall and on the side is a long slide, accessed by stone steps on the newly installed patio. Stunning, and I'm sure very expensive. I swim back to where Tabitha sits on her lounge chair.

"I wanted to tell you something else," Tabitha says, putting her hand up to shade her eyes from the sun. "About Anne."

"What? We were way off about her."

"I don't know. There's still something strange about her," she says. "When I was coming home from shopping with Lucy the other day, a cat ran across the road, and I had to stop my car in front of Anne's house to let it pass."

"Was it her cat? Gilbert?"

"What? No, it was a black cat. Anyway, her curtains were open, and she was standing by them talking to someone else in the room."

"Maybe she had friends over."

"There were no cars in her driveway, and it was almost midnight."

"She could have been on the phone."

"No, someone else was in the room," Tabitha insists. "I saw a shadow on the opposite wall in the living room. I couldn't see a face, but it was a shadowy figure with long hair. I think they were wearing a baseball cap too."

"Tabitha, so what? I don't see a big deal about this. She might have had a friend stay the night."

"Anne looked up, probably my headlights gave me away, and I don't think she realized her curtains were open. She closed them real fast."

"I don't like people peeping in my windows either," I reply.

Tabitha rolls her eyes. "I was not peeping, but it was strange. There is something off about Anne, and even though we know about Kim now, I still don't trust Anne."

"Was Grant's story about the work stuff true or was he making that up?"

"True." She pauses. "At least I think so. Anne could still be here to spy on him and us. Everything that happened does not make her innocent."

"Yeah, but it doesn't make her guilty either," I reply, turning to swim underwater.

The silence under the surface does little to quiet all the questions swirling around in my mind.

I shift in the cream and red vinyl train seats. It's midday on a Wednesday, just two days after my first appointment with the IVF doctor, so it isn't too crowded. Across from me, a young woman in her early twenties is scrolling through her phone and randomly taking selfies. Behind me is a haggard-looking woman with a toddler who keeps kicking my seat. Thankfully, the seat next to me is empty, so I move over. A well-dressed man sits in front of me and must be listening to an interesting podcast because random utterances like "That's right" or "Yes" spring from him at varying intervals.

My latte, half consumed, is clutched in my hand. I take a gulp of the now lukewarm goodness and stare out the window at the buildings and billboards we pass. I have to get some more tests done at the IVF doctor's and then am meeting Zach at the bank to go out to dinner.

The train hums along, and my mind hums too. I rather enjoy being alone with my thoughts. Sometimes I wonder who I would be if I wasn't a twin, only an individual. I doubt I'd be living in Little Beak. Would I be married to Zach? I don't think I'd own a bakery, even though I love it now. When I was younger, I always thought I'd be a veterinarian. Animals love me and I love them. Tabitha thought it was a stupid idea. I wanted to get a dog when we married, but Zach has allergies, or so he says: I remember him having a dog as a child and don't recall any allergies.

I guess everyone wonders what if this happened or that

happened, would my life be dramatically different, or would I be in a similar life? The old story of the road not taken.

My mind was still whirling after I left from discussing Kim's possible pregnancy with Tabitha. But once back at home I remembered our visit to the IVF clinic and had been buzzing with excitement at the new hope for me and Zach. But when he'd got back, Zach had been touchy on the subject, claiming he had been drained by his meeting and couldn't think about IVF then. We haven't been able to find a good time since.

I sigh, still thinking about my life in an alternative universe as a vet, married to a lumberjack. Might not be a bad life. Simpler than my current one.

SIXTEEN

TALIA

The moonlight filters through the tall bushes in our backyard. I sit at the patio table, drinking a hot tea with honey, hoping it will make me sleepy. With the lack of sleep I've been experiencing lately, I've been considering getting a prescription for sleeping pills; over the counter medication isn't doing the job.

The crisp night air causes me to pull my robe tighter against my body. Stars fill the sky above me, the skies clear and translucent, no remnants of the rain earlier in the day existing. A gentle breeze ripples the leaves in the tree by our patio, lending a comforting hum to the evening.

My conversation with Tabitha still plays in my mind. I'm surprised how well she is handling everything. She believes Grant is finished with Kim, but if Kim is pregnant it will be no such thing: She will be in their lives forever. Personally, I have my doubts that he is done with her now. Kim is not a regular-looking woman, more supermodel material, and in my opinion, the tidy and fast "things are over" speech Tabitha kept giving me was a bit forced. My emotions twist, torn in so many different directions, with my issues with Zach, IVF, and Tabitha's ongoing problems.

If I am honest, I expected Tabitha to react more to Grant's infidelity. Sure she was angry, but I thought she'd be much more aggressive, violent even; and I'm surprised that she handled things with Kim and Grant almost diplomatically. Very unlike her. Her reaction scares me a bit. Is it only the relative calm before the storm? How would I feel if it was Zach cheating on me with Kim? Hurt, confused, angry. Which emotion would take center stage? Probably hurt. I would want to know why he would risk our marriage for someone he barely knew. I doubt I'd be able to trust him again.

And then there's Anne. Curiosity swirls inside of me at who was at her house that night Tabitha mentioned. Strange too how the week prior I'd heard voices and clinking silverware from her back window. Surely, she had company, yet there was no car in her driveway.

Does Anne not live alone? Maybe someone lives with her. We only assumed she was on her own. Peculiar she would never mention it though, given how many times we've spoken. Surely, she'd want to introduce her housemate, and wouldn't that person want to be known?

Unless... she's hiding this person. I nearly shatter my mug, slamming it down on the glass patio table. This new thought crossing my mind shocks me. Another person may be living in the house next door. An anonymous person. I stare at the hedge between our house and Anne's. Who could it be?

Is it a woman, or a man? Tabitha's observation only reveals a shadowy figure, probably with long hair, wearing a baseball cap. Is it a friend, family, possibly a lover? Maybe even someone running from the law. The thought scares me. We could be living next door to a criminal! I've heard writers should write what they know; could Anne's mystery novels be somewhat true accounts? Maybe she's harboring a fugitive in her house. My mind spins again. I am never going to sleep if I don't get some pills and find out Anne's secret.

It's probably about one in the morning since I came out here shortly after midnight. About the same time Tabitha saw the shadowy form in the window at Anne's and about the same time I heard conversation and the clink of silverware from her window. Why didn't I think that was odd? Who eats dinner at midnight? Maybe this mystery person only comes out at night. Or maybe he, or she, is only allowed out at night. Could Anne be some sort of psycho keeping this woman prisoner in her house? Where is this person during the day? The questions keep hammering my mind.

I stand and make my way to the back of the bush row where I've made a hole in the shrubbery to observe Anne's back porch and yard. All remains silent. Two lounge chairs sit under a large oak tree in the center of the yard. The patio table has four cushioned chairs neatly tucked under the table and a book lies on top. The back glass patio door is covered with a privacy curtain, but dim light can be seen behind it. I strain my neck through the hole to get a better look.

The kitchen light flashes on. Anne stands at the window getting a glass of water from the sink faucet. Another figure moves beside Anne. Shadowy, away from the light, but another person, a person wearing a dark baseball cap. I'm not able to determine if it's a man or a woman.

The light goes off. Both figures disappear from my view.

SEVENTEEN

TALIA

"It's that time of year again," Claire says, walking in the front door of the cupcake shop. She holds up a large canvas grocery bag. "All the fall sprinkles were picked out; I got what I could find."

"Thanks, Claire," I say, taking the bag. "We've had more orders this year than any other."

"That's great! I swear the festival gets bigger every year. Everyone really enjoys it. My daughter is super excited about the dance-off competition. I made her such a cute outfit. Very purple and sparkly."

"How fun!" I exclaim. "I bet she'll love showing off her dance moves."

I take the bag into the back room and survey its contents. Not exactly everything I want, but I'll make it work. I look at the rows of cupcakes and two large cakes Tabitha baked last night that need decoration. Chocolate, vanilla, vanilla latte, chocolate chip, cookies and cream, lemon, an array of delicious flavors that need creamy, delicious frosting. Today will be busy.

No surprise there, since tomorrow is the Little Beak Harvest Festival held in the park in the town's square. Zach has entered the Chili Cookoff, a new addition this year, and he's certain he'll win with his recipe. Cole likes to compete in the children's sack racing, and he also loves the dunking tank. This year the principal of his school is going to be in it, and he's super excited. For Tabitha and I, we stay at our booth most of the time, selling cupcakes and we have many specialty orders. The Chamber of Commerce ordered a haunted house cake, which will take me some time to decorate; and Little Beak Preschool ordered a cake to be decorated as a giant spider; the bank wants a four-layer pumpkin cake with cream cheese, decorated like a pumpkin, plus numerous cupcake orders mean I'll be busy today.

I turn on my stand mixer, whipping up a creamy butter-cream, adding black food coloring to start on the spider cake. I want to get everything finished because I have to leave early today for an appointment. I like being busy today; it takes my mind off other things like the mysterious person I saw with Anne through her kitchen window a few days ago. I hid in the bushes the last two nights but didn't see anything else strange. I'm starting to feel like a psychopath creeping around in my backyard. Zach is wondering why I'm never in bed with him anymore. I want to tell him what I saw, but he's so consumed with his new job promotion I don't want to add more to his plate. I didn't even tell Tabitha about the person in the window. Something holds me back; I'm sure of what I saw but don't want to tell her. Not that it matters; she is hellbent that someone else was at Anne's house that night and doesn't trust her at all. She still thinks Anne has some sort of connection with Grant, and I'm sure everything will erupt at some point. I'll keep my infor-mation to myself, at least for now. I rather like having a mystery for myself to solve.

As I ice the cake an old song comes on the radio, and I start humming along. Zach and I have another appointment with the IVF doctor in two weeks. The next round of testing will be complete by then and they will go over all the results. I am still debating if this is the route I want to take. After a week of inde-cision, Zach said he'd go with whatever I want to do. I'm lucky to have such a considerate husband.

The back door opens, and Tabitha struts in, wearing tight black leggings and a purple yoga top. She whips off her over-sized sunglasses, shoving them in her purse and moves close to me.

"I have an idea," she whispers.

"Why are you whispering?" I ask.

"I don't want Claire to overhear," she says, her eyes barely an inch from mine.

"What is it?"

"Tomorrow at the festival, Anne was asked to do a book signing."

"How do you know?"

"Dan from the bookstore told me. Anyway, this is our chance."

"For what?"

"To search Anne's house, see what she's hiding."

"Or who," I mumble. I lay down my decorating tools and wipe my hands on the apron I am wearing.

"What?"

"Um... nothing. You mean break into her house? How would we get in?"

"The Edwards gave you an extra key for emergencies, right? You still have it?"

I'd completely forgotten about that, but, yes, I do. It's in an envelope in my kitchen drawer. They must have forgotten too, as they have never asked for it back. But we'd be breaking into someone's house, invading their privacy. I can't do that, can I? Anne hasn't even done anything. She's always been pleasant and a nice friend.

I nod. "I do, but I can't break into her house."

Tabitha hisses, "It's not breaking in if you have a key.

Besides, if you don't do it, I'll do it myself. I'll find the key in your house."

"I don't know. I guess I would be just using the key. It's not like we're going to break a window to get inside," I say, hesitantly.

I do not want to do this, but I can see how insistent Tabitha is being about the subject. If I don't go in with her, I have no doubt she'll steal the key and go in by herself. That may be worse.

"Exactly, and we know the Edwards didn't have a security system," Tabitha says, a smirk covering her face. "Who knows what we'll find in there. We'll tell Grant, Zach, and Cole that we have to come back here to get more cupcake orders, and Claire will run the stand at the festival. Nobody will be around; it'll be perfect. Are you in?"

"I guess," I say, my stomach feeling sick. We should *not* be doing this.

I walk into the office of Dr. Marcia Bales, an airy space of cream and pale muted greens, on the Upper East Side. A sleek, modern cream sofa sits in the center of the room, flanked with seafoam green club chairs. Covering the floor, a soft cream area rug. An unusual pod-like coffee table sits in the center of the rug. Large floor to ceiling windows overlook the city.

Dr. Bales sits in one of the chairs, as she did for the first session. She looks up from her laptop and smiles. She has dark hair cut in a short, stylish haircut and has sizable diamond earrings in her earlobes.

"Hello, Talia," she greets me warmly. She motions to the sofa and other chair. "Sit wherever you like."

I choose the other chair, feeling that lying on a psychiatrist couch is a bit cliché.

"Hello, Dr. Bales."

"How have you been?" she asks in a friendly tone.

"Okay, well, I'm having trouble sleeping," I say.

"I can write a prescription for sleeping pills. They may help," she replies. "But first, we should try to find the cause. What do you think is causing the insomnia?"

"Yes, I think a prescription is a good idea." I fiddle with the arm of the chair instead of answering her question.

Part of me detests coming to a psychiatrist. Am I that weak I can't handle my own emotions? The other part knows I need to talk to someone other than family or friends. A neutral party. There is nothing wrong with seeking help for any mental health issue, but I still struggle with it. It doesn't have anything to do with being weak or strong but rather understanding and finding solutions.

"How are things with your husband?"

"Okay," I reply. My concern this week has been more about Tabitha than Zach. In the last session I shared with Dr. Bales about Zach's ups and downs, the instability of his moods, something I've lived with for years.

"And your sister"—she looks at her laptop—"Tabitha."

"Not great. I feel like she's bullying me into doing something I don't want to do." I stare out the mass of windows to the city skyline. "Not that I'm surprised. She's been doing that our entire lives."

"Why do you continue to allow her to bully you?" Dr. Bales asks. "You are an independent person. You don't have to do what she tells you."

I sigh. In theory, she is correct, but she doesn't know Tabitha. I don't want to break into Anne's house. How am I even considering invading someone's privacy like that? But I will go along with it to keep an eye on Tabitha. I don't fully trust her.

"Do you trust your sister?" Dr. Bales asks.

My gaze goes directly to her. It's as if she reads my mind.

"I'm not sure," I reply.

That night, I still can't sleep, despite the sleeping pill I took two hours ago. I toss and turn while Zach sleeps peacefully beside me. Finally, I get up, shove my feet into the slippers by our bed and trudge downstairs.

I fetch a glass of water and stand at the kitchen island, slowly sipping it. I open the middle kitchen drawer, filled with pens, paper, and assorted junk, lifting a small white envelope from the back. Inside, the Edwards' house key.

I know why I can't sleep. I'm worrying about the break-in Tabitha and I plan to do tomorrow. Regardless of if I have a key, or not, it is still an invasion of Anne's privacy and her home.

Will I do it?

I'm not sure. Normally I'd say no, definitely not, but the lingering questions nag at me.

Is she hiding something? What if Tabitha is right about her?

I told Dr. Bales that Tabitha was bullying me into it, but I can't hide the truth from myself. I want to know. Does that make me a bad person, I wonder?

I shove the envelope back into the drawer. I look at the French doors and the wall of windows in our kitchen facing the backyard. Every blind tightly shut, the door securely locked.

I fill my water glass again and go into the bathroom down the hall from the kitchen, retrieving the bottle of sleeping pills from the vanity drawer that Dr. Bales prescribed. Just one more. I pop it into my mouth and wash it down with a gulp of water. Hopefully I'll sleep.

I place the glass into the deep kitchen sink and make my way over to the sofa. Snuggling under the warm chenille blanket, I close my eyes, relaxing myself and hoping for sweet slumber.

A sharp, insistent knock hammers on our front door. First,

the doorknocker clanging against the steel door, then fists pounding. Louder and louder. I start and jump off the sofa.

Who is at the door at this time of night?

I rush to peer out the peephole. Anne stands there, hair in a messy ponytail, wearing an oversized black hooded sweatshirt. She appears distressed. What is going on? I open the door.

"Anne, what...?"

"Come with me." She grabs my hand and runs.

I reluctantly follow, fearing my arm may be pulled out of its socket if I don't comply.

We fly across the front yard, around the corner, into her backyard, entering her house through the back door. We enter her kitchen.

A blonde woman sits on a kitchen chair, hands tied to the arms of the chair, her face beaten and bloodied. Her head hangs down. Her eyes closed.

She is unconscious.

"Anne!" I shriek, pulling away from her grasp.

"It wasn't supposed to go this far," Anne is saying. "Things got out of hand. It never should have gone like this. The plan was so much different."

"Call the ambulance!" I yell. "She's going to die. Call 911!"

Anne stares at me, a maniacal look on her face. Her eyes widen and her lips curve into a disturbing smile. "Why would I do that? I'm not done yet."

She lunges at me.

I scream and try to run out to the backyard, but she blocks the door. I run around the kitchen, and she chases me. I never should have come here. I've got to get out of this house. I scream again.

"Zach!" I yell at the top of my lungs. "Help!"

"He can't save you now!" Anne says, throwing off her sweatshirt, now wearing a blood-soaked T-shirt. "You're in my house."

"Stay away from me!" I yell, diving for her cell phone, lying on the kitchen table.

I fall, landing on the soft, cushioned floor in my family room. I open my eyes to a dim, quiet house. My house. The only light on is over the sink in the kitchen.

I was dreaming. Wow, what a dream.

My heart races and I stretch out on the floor. I don't have the strength to get up. Remnants of the dream still linger with me. I remain on the floor. Must have been that extra sleeping pill that spun such a terrifying dream.

Or is it a warning not to go into Anne's house tomorrow?

My eyes fly wide open.

I will not be sleeping again tonight.

EIGHTEEN

TALIA

The Little Beak Harvest Festival continues to grow every year. Most everyone in town comes to the festival, enjoying the live music, good food, games and socializing with friends and neighbors. Started about five years ago, something new is added every year to the festivities. This year it's the Chili Cookoff, into which Zach has entered his much-beloved chili recipe. Tabitha and I will make our move, but we have to wait until the chili winner is announced.

"You do make the best chili," Grant remarks, eating a second bowl.

"Thanks, Grant," Zach replies. "Family recipe."

"When do they announce the winner?" Tabitha asks. She looks at me expectantly. She is ready to go explore Anne's house.

"Any minute now," says Zach. He places the lid back on his chili pot and turns to Cole. "Then we'll go on the Ferris wheel."

"Yes!" Cole exclaims, eating another bite of the blue cotton candy he holds tightly in his small hand.

Our stand was busy most of the evening. The excuse to go get more cupcakes from the bakery won't be questioned by anyone. In fact, we'll have to remember to actually get some: We are almost sold out. My dream from last night remains embedded in my mind, disturbingly so. I hold reservations about going into Anne's house and snooping around, but I already promised Tabitha I'd do it. I know she won't let me go back on my promise.

The announcer comes over the loudspeaker. "And the winner of the Chili Cookoff is... Zach Conner!"

The crowd claps and a few whistles go out. I kiss Zach, congratulating him on his win, and take a picture of him with his red ribbon of honor. Now it's time to go.

We wave goodbye to the guys and make a beeline for our pink company van, Little Beak Sweets emblazoned on the sides. A few minutes ago we saw Anne happily signing books and the line of people waiting with books continually growing.

"OK." Tabitha is driving, her long hair up in a tight pony-tail. "You have the key?"

"Shit, I forgot it. I put it on the counter but forgot to bring it with me."

"Damnit, Talia," Tabitha mutters. "I guess it's not a big deal; you live next door so just run in and get it. Looked like Anne would be busy for a while."

I nod. "What exactly are we looking for in there?"

"Whatever, pictures, notes, letters, anything to do with us or anything odd."

"What if..."

"What?"

I clear my throat. "What if we find something else?"

"Like what?"

"Um... a body or a person?"

Tabitha slams on the brakes. "You think she has a *body* in the house?"

"Well, you saw that shadowy figure and I've heard someone there, but there's never a car in the driveway. Maybe someone is in the house."

"That's something I hadn't considered," Tabitha muses. She is quiet for a few moments. "OK, I don't think that's a possibility. Just stick to our plan."

"All right," I say.

We pull up to my house and park in the driveway. Adrenaline pumps through me now. I dash inside, grab the key, and Tabitha and I walk over to Anne's back door, gaining entry inside the attached garage. A quick survey of the space reveals nothing more than a lawnmower and some gardening tools.

We enter the house, closing the door behind us. A strong sulfur odor greets us, its pungent tentacles encircling us as we venture inside the structure. Tabitha and I stare at one another; eyebrows arching. We agreed earlier not to talk, in case someone is hiding inside Anne's house, as we didn't want any unnecessary noise to alert them. I continue to wonder endlessly about the identity of the person hiding in Anne's house, if such a person exists, and why he or she would be hiding.

We stand still for a few moments assessing the house, listening for any unusual sounds or movements. The round kitchen clock above the sink ticks slowly, its sound minimal, yet deafening in the dead silence of the house. The smell intensifies around us, and I move across the kitchen hoping to lessen the stench surrounding us. Nothing appears out of place in the kitchen, so we continue to walk through the house. The smell lessens as we enter the living room, and there's even less as we check out the office and bathroom, then the upstairs bedrooms, and bathrooms. A quick survey of closets and under the beds reveals nothing ominous.

Tabitha grabs my arm, her red manicured nails digging deep into my skin. She points to the floor.

A scuffling breaks the tense silence of the house, then a

squeak. Silence again. I look into Tabitha's hazel eyes, sparking with curiosity and a hint of fear.

Who is in the basement?

I point to the stairs leading downstairs. We both ready the nozzles on the small pink mace cans carried by each of us, in case of a confrontation. The steps are carpeted, reducing our noise as we creep, step by step, into the mostly dark basement. Only a dim glimmer of light flickers below, and I'm unsure of its source. Is someone waiting for us at the bottom of the stairs? I grip my mace can tighter.

Time seems to exist on another plane as we descend the staircase, encased by walls on both sides, unaware of what is lurking in the dimness below. I wish now I never agreed to come here. The smell from the kitchen wafts down behind us, the source still unknown.

We reach the bottom of the stairs and stop. The dim light comes from a flickering night light to the left of the stairway. A movement to the right causes us to jump and flatten against the wall. Out of the darkness, an orange cat emerges and runs past us up the stairs.

"Oh, Gilbert!" I exclaim. "I forgot about him!"

"Stupid cat!" Tabitha mutters, flicking on the light switch. Light floods the finished basement.

The stairs lead to a large family room with a beige sectional sofa, fireplace, large TV above it and a worn, but cozy, leather recliner to the side. An office/workout area is on the other side, along with a half bath, and the rest of the space is a large laundry room and storage area. We check all the places a person or a body may be hidden, but find none, thankfully.

"OK." Tabitha lets out a sigh of relief. "No bodies, so I'm going upstairs to look around. You check things out down here." She goes upstairs.

I give the family room a quick glance, nothing seeming interesting here, then move on to the storage room. I poke around boxes and plastic tubs, some from the Edwards, but some Anne's. One box holds an assortment of different colored yarns and knitting needles, along with two pretty knitted blankets. She has an entire plastic storage container of paperbacks, and a few hardcovers, of her books. I study the dark cover depicting an old, creepy-looking farmhouse, titled *The Secret*.

"Find anything?" Tabitha calls down the stairs.

"No," I reply, putting the book back into the bin and closing the lid. "Nothing."

I move over to the office space. A neat, modern-style black desk dominates the room; comfortable, ergonomic office chair in sleek black, printer, and basic office supplies fill the area. A bright turquoise hutch lined with books stands against the back wall, and next to it a long shelf with hooks, numerous sweatshirts and sweaters hanging from them. And on one peg, a dark blue cap.

I lift the cap and examine it. Plain, no logo on the front, canvas hat. Unremarkable. I drift back to the image I saw, or thought I saw, through the kitchen window. The shadowy person wearing a dark baseball cap. Was this the one?

An incoming text beeps on my phone. I glance at it. *Anne*. WTF, why is she texting me?? I read it.

Where are you?

Does she know we're here? I look around the room. Does she have cameras in here?

Three dots come up, then disappear.

I must answer. What am I going to say? Another message pops up from Anne.

Talia? I'm looking for you.

Fuck... I can barely breathe. I force myself to take a deep

breath and start to respond. My body shakes. Another text from her comes in.

> I'm behind you.

I scream and jump around. Nobody is there.

"What's wrong?" Tabitha comes rushing down the stairs.

"Anne is texting me! She said she was behind me!"

"What?" Tabitha grabs my phone and reads the texts. Another one comes in.

> Nope, wasn't you. Thought I was behind you in line at the French fry stand.

"You have to respond," Tabitha says.

"Give me my phone." I grab it from her and type out a quick text.

> We had to go get more cupcakes.

Three dots.

> OK, I'll catch up with you later.

I let out a loud sigh. My heart races and I think I'll be physically sick, my stomach churning so much. "We've got to get out of here, Tabitha," I say, running upstairs with my sister.

NINETEEN

TALIA

The media room in Tabitha's house is basically a mini movie theater. Plush red leather theater seating, soft black carpeting with white polka-dots, huge viewing screen, real working popcorn machine and a full bar at the back of the room. If you would have told us, as kids, we'd have our own private theater when we were adults, I'd have said you are crazy. And when we're in her media room, or movie theater, whatever you'd like to call it, we still act like kids sometimes. Kids that drink wine.

When Harry Met Sally plays on the screen today, one of our all-time favorite movies. The storyline reminds me of my relationship with Zach, since we were friends for years before becoming a couple after college, shortly before Tabitha and Grant's wedding.

"More wine?" Tabitha asks, holding the bottle.

"Please," I say.

She fills my empty glass snug in the recliner's built-in cup holder.

I shove a handful of popcorn in my mouth and down a gulp of wine. It's Monday, our day off, and we are discussing our findings after looking around Anne's house yesterday, specifically the strange photos. I'm sick of talking about it and sicker still of thinking about it, so I drink wine.

"This is the perfect movie," Tabitha remarks. "They know each other so well before they get together. Real friends. Best friends." A wistfulness hangs in her voice.

I look at her. Her hair is soft and loose, hanging long down her slim shoulders, and she still wears her workout clothes from the gym earlier in the day, same as me. She looks younger, like this, relaxed and a little messy, no preening around like she is most of the time. Times like this remind me of when we were younger, just having fun spending time together, watching movies, baking together, playing outside on the swings, and taking walks through the woods, sometimes with Zach, sometimes just the two of us. All good memories.

"Were you and Grant friends first before you started dating?"

She laughs. "Don't you remember? I slept with him on our second date. I mean, how can someone be just friends with a guy that looks like him."

"Hottie McHot," I say, both of us laughing.

"Yeah, McDreamy and McSteamy rolled together into one," Tabitha replies, still laughing.

"Oh, this is fun," I say. We needed a day like this, just sitting around laughing and being silly. We have some things to talk about, but for now I enjoy the fun.

I laugh again. "Zach and I were friends first."

"Zach is different. We talked about this before." She takes another gulp of wine. "I'd trust him with my life. We've known him forever."

"I know, right, just like the movie," I swoon.

"You know, I had a bit of a crush on Zach in high school," says Tabitha.

"You never told me! When?" I ask.

"Um... I guess ninth grade. Don't worry, it was just a silly crush. Didn't last long."

"I'm not worried. He had a crush on you too. You knew that, but I never knew you liked him."

"I liked him, but you loved him," she teases. "He was all yours."

I laugh. "I always had stronger feelings for him than you."

We are both tipsy and already on our second bottle of wine. It doesn't matter. Tabitha's housekeeper will pick up Cole from school and make dinner. Zach has a bank function and won't be home until late. Sometimes sitting around and talking and laughing is the best medicine for the soul.

"Yes, you have a love that will last," Tabitha says, slightly slurring her words.

"So do you," I reply.

"Do I? Is that why he had to bang some chick from the gym? And now she might be pregnant?" she asks. "How dumb is he?"

"I don't know."

"There's too much to think about, Talia. I'm going to work it out with Grant. I am. I want to be with him, and Cole needs him; but what am I going to do about Anne?"

"Why do you think she has those pictures?" I ask. I don't want to keep thinking about this, but my mind can't seem to move off it.

Tabitha took pictures of everything she found on Anne's desk in her bedroom. Surveillance-style pictures of Grant and Tabitha in their driveway. Me and Tabitha in front of Little Beak Sweets. Grant on the apartment stairs. Zach in the bank parking lot. There were more pictures, but Tabitha didn't have a chance to see them since I was screaming and she ran downstairs to see what about, and we had to leave after Anne texted me. I still can't believe she texted me while we looked through her house. It's so creepy. But, surprisingly, Tabitha was right:

Anne might be here for a reason other than writing books. Why else would she have those pictures of us?

Another possibility exists, though. Who is the person wearing the baseball cap that I saw in the window? Does he or she have a connection to Grant? The thought crosses my mind that the mysterious person may be Kim. Maybe she was friends with Anne previously and didn't want anyone to know. Could Kim be trying to keep tabs on Grant by involving Anne and her proximity to him? All I have are outlandish ideas at this point. Nothing that makes any sense.

"She must be running surveillance on him for someone. Those pictures look like something you'd see on a cop TV show," Tabitha says. "Maybe Anne works for the FBI."

"The FBI? Why would the FBI be surveilling Grant? And why would they want pictures of us, too? None of this makes any sense. Is Grant doing something illegal at work?"

"I don't know, Talia! I don't know anything! He barely tells me anything. All he said was something strange was going on at work. How should I know? It might be something illegal. I don't think people are watched if they are following the rules," Tabitha yells. "Maybe I should just get a divorce. He doesn't even talk to me. I'm his wife and he has this whole secret life. Affairs, people following him around, what the hell."

I nod. "You could divorce him."

She shakes her head. "I don't want to do that. I love him, but I am angry at him. I have so many feelings all mixed together and it's making me crazy."

I reach over and put my arm around her. "I know and I'm here for you. We'll get through this, and we'll get some answers."

TWENTY

TABITHA

I close the door to the media room and walk outside onto our new patio. Talia left about an hour ago and it will be an hour before Amy, our housekeeper, brings Cole home from school. The calm trickling of the waterfall cascading into the kidney-shaped pool soothes my frayed nerves. A little bit of solitude will be good for me to try to sort out my feelings.

My head aches slightly, a wine headache. I sip some water and sit in a lounge chair in a sunny spot by the pool. I consider going in the hot tub but don't feel like going back into the house to put on my bathing suit. The comfortable lounge chair will have to do for now. This afternoon was so much fun. Watching old movies, hanging out with Talia, being silly and really sharing my feelings with her was a relief for me. Giggling about silly stuff made me think of when we were kids or teenagers, just having a good time; and the problems we faced back then were minimal compared to what is going on in my life now.

I wasn't sure if she'd go for the idea of using the key to enter Anne's house. My hunch was she was going to act pious about it and I'd have to snatch the key and do the dirty work myself. But she actually seemed as interested in checking things out in

Anne's house as I did. She threw me for a loop when she mentioned the chance of a body, or a person, being hidden in Anne's house. That possibility never crossed my mind, and I am thankful Talia wasn't right. And, finally, Talia agreed with me that Anne harbors a secret. Those pictures are solid proof, however they turned up. Proof that Anne is a danger to all of us.

Talia didn't like what we found, but I expected it. Sometimes I wonder what it would be like to go about in life like Talia. She floats about acting like she's so much smarter and better than me. She doesn't realize the life she lives today is because of me. I step aside when something is important to her. I want her to be happy, but I also want happiness and for her to appreciate how much I give to her. I must admit, she doesn't know about everything I've done in the past, but all of it is needed to keep her happy and close to me. Sometimes I think I'm the only one who truly values our twin bond and nurtures it to last throughout our lives. I doubt we'd be in the life we enjoy now if it wasn't for me, but Talia never recognizes it. I'm always the one looking out for her, looking ahead to see if the seas are calm for her and taking care of any wakes in her path. I fend for myself, I have to, it's my nature. People take care of Talia, like me, like Zach. We do it because we love her, but she remains blissfully unaware of all we do for her. My love for Talia is deep, but I couldn't sacrifice everything for her. I deserve to be happy too.

When Grant and I moved to Little Beak I was consumed with major house renovations and decorating, but as things calmed, I sank into a deep depression. Some days I could barely get out of bed; I was miserable. I missed Talia. We talked often, but she was hours away and I needed her with me. Talking on the phone, or texting, even video chat wasn't the same as having her physically near me. We had been together our entire life, for the most part, and it didn't seem right that she wasn't close by, that I couldn't just go over to her house, or hop in the car and go out to lunch. I appeared to be the only one experiencing this withdrawal from her presence, though. She seemed fine, content with a daily phone call, usually initiated by me, but I craved her presence in my life. And it made me so mad that she didn't seem to crave mine.

Another trait of Grant's I've always admired is his generosity. If someone needs something, he'll be the first one to offer it. He didn't give a second thought when I suggested we give Talia and Zach the money for a down payment on the house next door; I knew they wouldn't be able to afford it otherwise. He knew it would make me happy, and was glad to do it. And Grant got Zach the job at the bank, in which he excels. I had my sister living next door and the depression lifted. The years passed and while the depression never returned, other emotions have surfaced. Talia has never needed me like I need her. I don't know why, but living close, and working with her, has shown me that she will never change. I think she enjoys living in Little Beak with us, but I also think she'd be just as happy somewhere else without me. I never was as important to her as she is to me. For some reason, I thought that may change as we got older, but she continues to take me for granted. Yet I am always there making life good for Talia.

I have had a lot on my mind lately, so I'm looking forward to the upcoming weekend. Grant, Cole and I will be joining Grant's family at their Hamptons compound to celebrate his father's sixty-fifth birthday. It will be a nice distraction to get away, spend a little time by the ocean, and just relax and spend time together as a family. The family compound allows plenty of space so that the only actual time I'll need to see his family will be at the party. Otherwise, everyone does their own thing. Grant's family, particularly his parents, are not fans of me. They thought he married "trailer trash" even though I have never lived in a trailer. I overheard them talking about me when we were dating many years ago and their coolness toward me has never warmed. In a way, I can see their point: while I like to act like an uppity society girl, and certainly enjoy all its amenities, that character isn't my true self.

Yes, reconnecting with Grant and spending time with Cole as a family will be the best medicine that we can give to each other. Family means everything to me, and I will do anything to work through our problems and find our happy ending.

TWENTY-ONE

TALIA

Claire runs a hand through her balayage bob and picks up her box of cupcakes from the crowded counter. She grins at me, her eyes bright. "Well, the girls will be happy I brought these home for dessert. I'll be a hit at the sleepover."

"Oh, hope you have a fun night!" I say.

"Thanks, you have a good evening, too." She smiles and waves, walking out the door. "See you tomorrow."

The bakery silences in her absence, only me and the numerous cupcake orders lining the counter behind me waiting to be picked up for the weekend. I'm working until five tonight, normally Tabitha's shift. She, Grant and Cole are headed out to the Hamptons for the weekend. I glance at the giant cupcake clock on the wall behind me. They are probably leaving about now. I hope they have a good time; some family time would be good for all of them. And the way Tabitha describes the family compound in the Hamptons, they will have plenty of private space despite the presence of the rest of Grant's family.

I don't mind working. Zach is at a bank conference for the weekend; he said he wouldn't be home until Sunday afternoon. So I'm on my own, no husband, no sister. I relish the freedom to do whatever I want, although I do need to work tomorrow until two, but, then the world is my oyster. Some people are bothered by spending time alone, like Tabitha. She likes to be in the middle of everything. Groups, clubs, outings, whatever is going on she wants to be the center of it. Even if she has a day to herself, she still wants to spend it with me, never just her. I'm not one of those people. I love alone time. No conversation, no answering questions, no tedious day to day nonsense. Just enjoyable time spent by yourself with your mind and your creative pursuits. Truly a pleasure to be cherished. Tonight, I'll work on a blanket I've been knitting. A Christmas blanket in a vibrant red.

Today was quiet, which is nice, but makes the day drag on a bit. A few orders and walk ins, but the busiest time will be in about an hour when everyone stops in for their prepaid orders. I have already baked and decorated everything needed for tomorrow morning, so I sit down at one of our tables, nursing an iced coffee, and scrolling through my phone.

A text pops up.

From Anne.

> Would you like to go out to dinner tonight?

I pause. Would I?

> Sure, what time?

> Six? I can drive.

> I won't be done at the bakery until about 5:30. It'll have to be somewhere casual, maybe Antonio's? I can meet you there.

> OK, see you then.

Interesting. I've gone the entire week without running into

Anne. I haven't sneaked around the yard. My new prescription sleeping pills are working, so I've slept in bed with my husband. No bad dreams, or rather, nightmares. A good night's rest is a welcome change for me. I need a clear head with all that is going on in my life right now. I'm trying to forget Anne exists. Those pictures threw me for a loop. If I don't see her, she doesn't see me. I don't want her to see me.

Now I'm going to dinner with her.

Antonio's is the perfect pizza place in town. Delicious food, loud music, always a busy environment with people coming and going, especially on a Friday night. Yes, a perfect place to meet a woman who is stalking me and my family.

"Talia!" Anne calls. She sits in a booth in a small alcove toward the back of the restaurant, near the bathrooms and the back door. Not the busy main area I would have chosen. Perfect to stuff me full of pizza and capture me as I waddle out the rear door.

"Hi, Anne!" I force cheerfulness. I planned on getting here earlier to pick the table, but Dan from the bookstore droned on forever when he picked up his order for book club tonight.

I join her in the booth. She excuses herself to use the bathroom and is back a few minutes later.

She sits down and smiles, a wide one accentuating her very straight, very white teeth. She must have had an excellent orthodontist as a child. Anne is quite lovely. Her long, dark, curly hair falls loose tonight, and the emerald-green blouse she is wearing accentuates her wide-set green eyes. A delicate emerald and diamond ring adorns her right ring finger.

"What a pretty ring," I compliment. I lightly touch it and lift her hand over. "Do the diamonds go all around the band?" I stop, noticing a scar from the top of her palm down to mid palm. I allow her hand to rest on the table.

"Yes," she says, pulling her hand away and putting it under the table. "Diamonds all around."

"Beautiful," I murmur, the image of the scar stirring an old, uncomfortable memory. One I haven't thought of in years and wish I could erase from my mind. I brush it away.

"I'm so glad you could join me tonight," Anne says. "It's been a bit since I've seen you. I tried to catch up with you at the festival last week, but we never crossed paths."

"Oh, yes, it's a busy event for my sister and I."

"How is Tabitha?"

"She's well, her and her family are going to the Hamptons this weekend."

"Ooh, that sounds fun. A little ocean therapy is good for everyone."

"And my husband has a work conference this weekend. So, I'm all alone," I say, without thinking.

Great, I just admitted to the woman stalking me that I'm alone all weekend. Plenty of time to hide the body before someone realizes I'm missing. I'm such an idiot. A nervous giggle escapes me. I grab the menu.

"How nice. A quiet weekend for you," she remarks, cocking her head to the left. A fizzle of familiarity trickles through me. I shake off the odd feeling.

"Hmm... so what are you getting?" I ask, surveying the menu.

"Cheese ravioli," she says. "What about you?"

"A five-cheese personal pizza, cauliflower crust."

"I never tried cauliflower crust; I think I'll get that too."

"I love it," I say, closing the menu.

The waitress comes around for our orders and quickly returns with our drinks and salads.

"I am busy this weekend though," I say. "I work at the bakery tomorrow and then my afternoon yoga class at the gym."

"Sounds fun. I used to do yoga a lot but got out of the habit. Do you mind if I join you tomorrow?"

"Uh, yeah, sure. That would be fun."

"Great, I'll see you there. What time?"

"Two thirty."

Anne nods and proceeds to eat her salad. This dinner is a disaster. Now she knows I'm home alone and she's joining me for yoga tomorrow. I'm going to shut my mouth now.

She stabs a piece of broccoli. "Oh, I made broccoli last week and overcooked it. The entire house stank for a day or so. It was terrible."

I nod. That's the stink in the kitchen when we were in her house. At least that's explained.

"How's the writing coming along?" I ask.

"Pretty good. I'm more than halfway through the manuscript. The words are flowing well."

"Wonderful. I want to read your books," I say. "Zach read your first book and really enjoyed it."

"Oh, did he?" she remarks, an edge in her voice. She looks away. She reaches into the black tote bag next to her, pulling out a paperback copy of *The Secret*, with the creepy farmhouse on the front cover: the same book I saw in her basement. She hands it to me. "Here, I wanted to give this to you. I signed it."

I accept the book. "Thank you. That's very thoughtful."

"Sure, you're welcome." She grins. "A lot of time and research goes into a novel. Some research people may not expect is involved with writing a book."

"Like what?"

"Just watching people, their habits, different personalities." She pauses and looks directly at me. "Sometimes I take pictures."

"Of what?" I squeak. Trepidation trickles through me.

She knows we were in her house.

She knows.

"People just living their everyday lives. Looking at the pictures sometimes helps me progress with my story," she says nonchalantly.

I nod and chew my salad. This wasn't a friendly dinner. She must know we were in her house and saw the pictures. She probably even saw me looking at this book in her basement.

Does she have cameras installed in her house, or is this just an odd coincidence? But if she does have cameras and saw us, why wouldn't she just come out and say it?

Or is this part of a game she is playing with us?

TWENTY-TWO

TABITHA

Antonio's buzzes with patrons all getting their Friday night pizza fix. Grant got home late from work, so we decide to leave early Saturday morning. He is tired and doesn't feel like driving and I don't care either way. It's less time I have to spend with his mother. The family compound is quite large and spacious, but I doubt any space is large enough to avoid his mother completely. I said I'd grab a pizza for dinner, since our housekeeper has the week off, and Grant stayed home with Cole.

I make my way up to the counter, tell them my order number, and sit to wait a few minutes while they assemble it. I survey the area for a place to sit, but none is available, so I linger by the counter. I glance to the back of the restaurant, seeing a recognizable woman in a pink T-shirt with our cupcake logo, Little Beak Sweets, on the back. Talia.

Who is she here with? I strain my neck to see her slide into a booth set into an alcove toward the back. I wonder why she's sitting all the way back there. I can't see the other occupant of the booth, or if there is another person, until someone gets up and goes to the bathroom. Anne.

What the hell is she doing here with her? Unreal. Especially after what we found in her house! Anger surges through me and I feel heat rushing to my face. Damn it, Talia. She always does this to me. These secret friendships and excluding me—not that I want to be friends with Anne because I do *not*. Could Talia be working with Anne? Talia thought we'd have left for the Hamptons by now. She'd never expect me to be here getting a pizza. What kind of conversation could she be having with Anne?

"Number eighty-one," the guy at the counter calls. "Large pepperoni."

My order. I watch Anne walk out of the bathroom, her gaze meeting mine. No wave or acknowledgment of any kind. Just a dead stare directly at me. Her head cocks to the left and her lips pucker slightly as she sits down in the booth with Talia. Chills ripple through me at the familiar movement.

Just like...?

Impossible. A memory flashes in my mind, but I shut it down. I will not think about it. I wait a moment to see if Anne will tell Talia I'm here. A moment passes, then another. Nothing.

"Number eighty-one!" the guy calls again.

I grab my pizza and go out the door to my SUV. I sit in the driver's seat and text Talia.

> What are you doing?

Three dots. Nothing.
A message appears.

> Not much. How's the Hamptons?

I fling the phone on the passenger seat.
Can I trust my sister?

. . .

I didn't answer Talia. Now, as we stop at a quaint diner on the way to the Hamptons on Saturday morning, at Cole's request, waiting for our breakfast to arrive, another text from her pops up.

Hey, how's it going?

I stare at it, unsure if I want to answer.

"Who's that?" Grant asks, taking a sip of his orange juice.

"Talia," I reply.

"Aren't you going to answer her?"

"Later, I just want to enjoy breakfast with my two favorite guys," I say, smiling at Cole.

"Is that me and Daddy?" he asks, a big grin covering his face.

"Yes, it is," I say. "Oh, here comes your chocolate chip pancakes."

Cole's eyes widen at the tall stack of pancakes and side of bacon.

Grant looks at me. "I'm glad we're getting away for a few days. We needed some family time, just the three of us."

Cole is already working on his food. Grant reaches out and squeezes my hand. I squeeze back, staring into those gorgeous blue eyes. "I have everything I need right here. My family. Our family."

Love fills my heart in that moment. Grant and I will be fine. Everything will work out for us, and we'll continue to be the loving family we have always been. Cole deserves that and so do I.

TWENTY-THREE

TALIA

I say a prayer of relief when the sun begins filtering through the fabric blinds of our bedroom. Sleep proved fitful at best, but mostly nonexistent as I tossed and turned despite checking that all my doors were locked several times and even locking the bedroom door. I engaged the security system we recently installed, but rarely use. I wasn't taking any chances; I wanted to be securely locked in my own house, safe and sound.

That didn't keep me from peering from the side bedroom window late last night when I heard a noise outside...

Anne's garage is open, and she's fumbling around in the trunk, then she puts a black suitcase inside and slams it shut. She turns and stares over toward our backyard. Does she know I've been watching her from there? Probably. Or maybe Gilbert has wandered over into our yard again. I hope it's as simple as that.

I press myself flat against the wall and continue to watch through the exposed curtain at the side. I do *not* want her to see me. I'm already shaky about that dinner and her revelation about the pictures.

Anne stares for a bit, then casually strolls over to the row of tall bushes separating our property. She goes to the exact spot where the dead branches lend an unobstructed view of the other side.

Oh, my heavens, she knows I've been watching her. She knows where I watch her. She's watching *me*!

I continue to monitor her. After a few moments, she walks to the back of the shrubbery line, directly to the other bush I so meticulously trimmed to afford me an unobstructed view of her property. Again, she bends down and stares through the hole into *my* backyard!

I run back to our bedroom and lock the door. My labored breathing does little to calm my frayed nerves. She knows I watch her, and she must be watching me when I'm unaware. How did I not notice this? I've been vigilant in my surveillance of her. When did I become an object of *her* interest? Now I'm a prisoner in my own home. What does she want from me? Visions of the blonde woman in my dream spring to me. It wasn't real. Just a figment of my imagination fueled by too many sleeping pills. I was inside her house and the only other living thing in there was her cat, Gilbert. Unless... the person was hidden away. No, *stop*, I'm losing my mind now. I need to just focus on the facts. I grab my phone to see if Tabitha has texted back. Nothing. That is odd too. I want to tell her about Anne and dinner tonight, but don't want to ruin her family weekend. I decide to try tomorrow...

And, finally, now it's tomorrow. I get out of bed and head to the bathroom to shower and start the day. The warm water rolling down my body is a welcome distraction and I linger longer than normal, enjoying the warmth and sound of running water. I hear a text beep from my bedroom. I dry off, moisturize, and put on my robe. I stare in the mirror, wiping away the steam. I look tired, my hazel eyes sporting more flecks of green than brown, my skin greedily absorbing the applied moisturizer. I add some eye cream, trying to hide the darkness under them.

Sleep, or a lack of in my case, does a number on your skin. My long, honey-blonde hair has left more than a few strands in the bathroom sink.

The text beeps again. I go to retrieve my phone. Anne.

Sorry, I can't make yoga today. Something came up. Raincheck?

Good. I type a quick reply.

Sure, no problem.

Anne likes my reply with an emoji.

I put my phone down and sigh. One less thing to think about today. Nothing happened with Anne, nothing completely disturbing. Weird, sure, but am I really in any danger from her, or is it my paranoia spinning out of control? I need to keep myself grounded and not go off on tangents that may not be reality. I had issues with this in the past. Focus on the present and the facts, leave the rest of it to the side. I grab my phone again. Nothing from Tabitha. I type a quick message to her and wait. Nothing.

What's going on, Tabitha?

The workday flew by and, before I know it, I'm closing the shop, doing my yoga class, and heading home. Yoga is a welcome stress reliever and by the end of the hour-long session, my muscles and mind feel stretched, strong, and healthy. I drive past Anne's house, and everything appears quiet. The garage door is closed, curtains drawn, no activity, for which I'm thankful. She's probably in her office writing; hopefully she'll stay there. Tonight should be peaceful and restful, exactly what I need.

I park my car in the garage and quickly hit the opener to

close the door. All I want is a little snack, shower, and to crawl into bed. I throw my purse on the kitchen table and warm up some leftover chicken noodle soup. I stand at the counter eating my soup and sipping water. Tabitha still hasn't texted me back, so strange.

I wonder why Anne couldn't make yoga today when she's the one who suggested it. Something must have come up, but what? I don't know much about Anne's personal life. I know she doesn't have any brothers or sisters and that her parents have passed. Is she seeing anyone? Who are her friends? A bit odd that the numerous times we've talked, none of those topics came up, yet she knows all about my life. I take another spoonful of soup. I need to talk to Tabitha. I pull out my phone and call her. It rings until it goes to voicemail. I send a text.

> What's going on with you? Text me back or call.

I watch my phone, slowly finishing my soup. Fifteen minutes pass, thirty minutes pass, nothing. She's ignoring me. She does that from time to time. She gets mad at me for the dumbest things. I act like it doesn't bother me, but it does.

Whatever.

I check all the doors, twice, set the security system, take a shower, swallow my sleeping pills and crawl into bed. I lie there calm, welcoming a restful slumber, still feeling tranquil and rested, ignoring any type of negative intrusion on my thoughts.

It doesn't come.

I must have dozed off sometime, but at one in the morning I'm wide awake. I stay still and silent, staring at the ceiling once again, wishing I could fall back to sleep. I count the strands of moonlight filtering in through the blinds two or three times until I tire of its monotony. I glance at my phone on the night-stand. A missed call from Zach, but that is it.

I fling back the covers and put on my robe. I pad down the hall to the side bedroom and peer out at Anne's house. Everything appears dark and nondescript, certainly nothing to worry about there; either she is asleep, writing in the basement, or not at home. No noise from there tonight. Garage still shut, curtains drawn, no lights visible. Is she home? If not, where did she go? I can't help but wonder.

If she's in her office in the basement, I won't be able to see the basement lights from here, but I can see them from the back-yard. Why do I need to check? Maybe she went to bed early like me. However, it would be unusual. Anne seems to be a night owl, at least from my observations.

Should I go check?

I ponder. Maybe just a quick look. I put on my slippers and grab my mace. I move quickly down my stairs, open the French door to the patio and listen. Quiet, except the Millers' dog barking a few houses down, but that is normal. I clutch my mace and walk onto the patio.

What am I doing?

Last night I locked myself in my bedroom, now I'm voluntarily sneaking around outside to see if Anne's home. No wonder she's spying on me. I'm probably a bigger nut job than her. This week's appointment with Dr. Bales is going to be intense.

The moon hangs high and is partially obscured by clouds. The dog barking quiets, and the only noise left is the chirping of tree frogs in unison, although much quieter than their summer song. The stillness welcomes me, yet uneasiness fills me as I walk the short distance to my bush lookout in the back. I lean in to peer through the open space. I close my eyes for some reason, then the thought of seeing Anne's eyes staring back at me through the bushes gives me a start. My eyes open wide now.

The view of Anne's backyard is pretty much the same: two lounge chairs by an oak tree, chairs neatly tucked under a patio table—no book on top this time. The house completely dark. No lights from the basement windows. No lights anywhere, only blackness.

Is Anne asleep?

Or is the house empty?

TWENTY-FOUR

TALIA

My phone rings and rings. My head is in a fog, and I struggle to wake up out of my stupor. My hand fumbles around the nightstand until I manage to fling it onto the floor. The phone stops ringing for a moment, then begins again. My eyes are lead shades I force open; the extra sleeping pill I took last night really worked its magic. I may take another tonight and sleep the whole night. What a glorious treat. I glance at the clock. Ten in the morning.

I snatch up the phone. Tabitha's calling. It's about time.

I answer. "Where have you been?"

She's crying on the other end of the phone. Deep sobs.

"What's wrong? What happened?" I ask, softening my voice.

"Grant..." she wails. "Grant is dead."

"What? How?" Grant's dead, how can that be possible?

"Hit and run this morning. The police were here. He's... gone."

"OK." I jump out of bed. "I'm coming there. What's the address?"

She gives it to me, and I hang up the phone. I scramble

getting clothes on and putting a few items in an overnight bag. I don't know if she'll want to stay there or come home right away. I grab a bottle of water from the fridge and a granola bar from the pantry, then I'm on the road.

As I drive, her words repeat in my mind. It seems unreal that handsome, strong Grant could be dead. I try to think back to the last time I saw him. Just last week, at the harvest festival. Last week, when we prowled around Anne's house; it seems a lifetime ago. Grant is dead. The words ring in my ears but make no sense to me.

Even in my haste, I sneak a peek at Anne's house before I leave. Everything appears locked up, as it had yesterday: closed garage, pulled curtains, no sign of life. I think of the black suitcase she put into her trunk the night before: Is she planning on staying somewhere for a while? But why didn't she tell me she would be gone? Possibly because she didn't want me snooping around her house since she'd be away. That is a definite possibility. Another thought sprouts in my mind. Could Anne have been involved in Grant's hit and run? But what reason would she have to do such a thing? Could she and Grant have a secret relationship, unknown to us? She had photos of him, and she used to live in Manhattan, where he worked every day and where his parents live. Maybe they knew each other before she moved to Little Beak. Another illicit affair, possibly?

No, I will not speculate into unknown territory. Just stick to the facts that I know. Grant was killed by a hit-and-run driver hours away. How would Anne know Grant was in the Hamptons? Then I remember.

I told her.

My stomach churns. What if Tabitha's hunch is correct? If Anne is watching Grant for some reason, maybe had a vendetta against him for something, it would be an opportunity for her to strike. How can I be so stupid? I should have kept that information to myself. Grant's dead, leaving my sister a widow and Cole without a father and, if it was Anne, it's my fault.

The Nortons' Southampton compound is massive. The structure stands majestically among well-manicured shrubbery mixed with lush gardens filled with bright flowers and stone fountains, overlooking the Atlantic Ocean, stunning views in either direction. I have no idea how many square feet the house is, but it's huge. Palatial. I can see what Tabitha meant when she said there's plenty of private space for everyone. Plus, an enormous pool area, dual gable pool house, and guest cottage that could have easily been someone's main house, not to mention tennis court, basketball court, and an art studio that Grant's mother putters around in. She makes very pretty clay pots and paints the occasional floral scene. Being filthy rich certainly has advantages.

The housekeeper lets me in and directs me to the pool area. As I walk through the silent house, my shoes echoing on the tile floor, I do not encounter anybody else. I can't imagine how Grant's parents are dealing with everything that has happened.

Tabitha and Cole are at the large rectangular pool overlooking the ocean. The tranquil setting boasts two patio tables by the pool and several lounge chairs among the stone planters overflowing with colorful flowers, spilling out onto the concrete. Large white umbrellas provide shade to the various areas, much needed during a hot summer season. My sister lies on a white lounge chair in a black lace cover up, and large oversize sunglasses hide her eyes. Grant's sister, Ashley, lies on the lounge chair next to her, wiping her eyes; a large tissue box sits between them and a pile of used tissues beside it. Ashley is as blonde and blue-eyed as Grant but lacks his charm and attraction. She isn't unattractive, but so dull she seems almost blank when you try to have a conversation with her. She always appears a bit blah, bland as white bread, with a personality to match. The only exception is when she talks about the law; she's a lawyer—she perks up talking about various regulations and statues that I don't find particularly interesting; but at least something excites her. I don't care to spend much time with her, not that I have had a reason to do so; the only time I see her is at Tabitha's house—and she stopped inviting her over for dinner parties a long time ago. Now, Cole splashes around in the spacious pool. My guess is that Tabitha hasn't told him yet. Although, I see him watching her, and us, carefully. He's likely picked up on the somber vibes around him.

"Aunt Talia!" Cole waves, seeing me approach.

"Hi, Cole." I wave to him, and he goes back to swimming. I go to Tabitha and embrace her.

She stands and turns her back so Cole won't see and sobs on my shoulder. "Oh, Talia, I couldn't tell him. I can't tell Cole."

"I know." I hold her. "I'm so sorry."

We stand, holding each other for a few minutes, and then Ashley breaks the silence.

"Doughnuts," she says bluntly.

I look at her. She really is a dud. "What?"

She turns to me and lowers her sunglasses, blue eyes staring at me, reddened by crying. "Doughnuts."

I stare at her. "Yes, what about doughnuts?"

Tabitha sits back down on the lounge chair, checks if Cole is within earshot, which he isn't. "Grant went out to get those specialty doughnuts they have here. You know how much Cole loves them; we always get them when we're on vacation as a treat. He was hit by a car in the parking lot when he left the store."

I rub her back. I don't know what to say.

· · ·

The ride home is silent. Cole falls asleep soon after we start driving. I glance in my rearview mirror and smile at his peaceful slumber. His little blond head tips over and soft breaths escape him. Tabitha told him about Grant, but I'm not sure he fully understood what she was saying, but in time he will. Tabitha just sits staring out the window, mute.

We stayed over last night. I called Zach to let him know what happened and that I'd be home on Monday. Shocked, as we all are, he asked if he should come out, too, but there is no need. We handled things here; there wasn't much he could do that wasn't already being done. The discussion over where to send Grant's body for burial proved heated. Tabitha wanted Little Beak, but his parents insisted he be buried in the family mausoleum in Brooklyn. All the Nortons were buried there; Grant could be no exception. Tabitha relented when his mother became hysterical and his father told her there was room for her and Cole to be buried there too, one day. This wasn't a subject she thought she'd be dealing with at thirty-two years old and she said she didn't want to fight about it, so she gave in.

Grant's body will be transported there today. The police have no leads on the driver of the car, only that the car is a stolen Honda from Long Island. The person is unable to be identified at this point because they wore a ski mask, dark hooded sweatshirt, sunglasses, and gloves. It's unknown if it was a man or woman.

Everyone is numb, in shock, and after Grant's arrangements are made, there's nothing to talk about. Tabitha will go to the funeral home on Wednesday to do the burial arrangements and to set a funeral date. I still can't believe Grant's gone. The whole situation seems unreal to me, to all of us. Grant was so healthy and full of life, for him to be here one day and gone the next, absurd. I will miss him, and my heart aches for Tabitha and Cole.

As I drive along the highway, Tabitha falls asleep too,

leaving me alone with my thoughts, which come back to Anne. My gut says she hadn't been home since Friday night, probably when I saw her put that black suitcase into her trunk. No sign of life existed on Saturday or Sunday morning. I try to remember anything that indicates her being at home but come up with nothing. Wherever she went, it was unplanned, it would appear; otherwise why not mention a planned trip to me on Friday? And why make plans to do yoga with me on Saturday if she wasn't going to be around? Is it a bit convenient that we find pictures of Grant and us, all of us, in her house and now Grant is killed in what appears as a targeted hit and run? Where's the logic in this scenario of Anne being the driver of the car? What can she possible gain by killing Grant? Was she also having an affair with him? Perhaps jealousy took over and she couldn't stop herself when she found out about Kim and Grant. She was acting strange that day we went out for breakfast and Grant was home from work. Maybe that's the real reason she had the pictures of us: she was stalking Grant, keeping tabs on him because of their relationship.

Could Anne have been in the Hamptons yesterday morning?

TWENTY-FIVE

TABITHA

The damp October day hangs heavy with dark clouds, only a wisp of sky visible between them. Rain threatening but never materializing over the crowd of mourners. Clothed in black, we walk solemnly to the Gothic-style family mausoleum with intricate pointed etching adorning each post of the structure. Only a slight murmuring is heard among funeral goers, and we wait for the burial service.

We sit in the vestibule of the mausoleum, such a dreadful, suffocating place. Cole tight by my side, so handsome in his little black suit. Others shuffling inside, then the pallbearers enter the doorway with the casket. They carry it inside and place it within the open crypt.

The pastor says a few words of comfort, and I stare at the dark, shiny casket, unable to believe Grant's inside of it, and I'll never see him again in this life. I feel so old suddenly, and weary. I never could have imagined this is the direction my life would take me. Widowed at thirty-two with a six-year-old son.

Alone.

My thoughts travel back to that sunshine-filled day in Central Park when Grant proposed to me. Only eleven years ago, but it feels like a lifetime. It was autumn, not the gray kind of day like this. No, the crisp, fresh day with gold and fire red leaves falling from the trees. A day filled with hope and anticipation of the beauties it held. That dizzying feeling of pleasure and enjoyment we wish we could bottle and keep engaging when our dark days crept in. We packed a picnic lunch and went to The Pool in Central Park, one of my favorite spots, and the most beautiful place in the park. Secluded and not too touristy, I loved sitting on the grassy hill under the weeping willows overlooking the water. A quiet spot in an always busy city. The fall colors surrounding us were spectacular.

We ate our lunch, and he got down on one knee and proposed. I can still feel the excitement inside me when he slipped the ring on my finger, and remember his lips on mine when we kissed. That's how I will remember Grant, on a sunshine-soaked afternoon when everything was possible for us, and love bound us together.

Tears stream down my face.

TWENTY-SIX

TALIA

I stretch my legs out on the sofa and watch Zach pour a scotch and grab a bag of pretzels from the pantry. "Do you want something?" he calls from the kitchen.

"One of those," I say, pointing to his drink. I snuggle into our sofa as he pours another. He walks over, hands me the drink, and sits down with a sigh.

"What a day," he comments, taking a drink.

"Yeah," I agree, doing the same.

"I know it's a cliché, but it really goes to show you, life is never predictable. You never know what is in store for you. Anyone who says they know what they're doing in life is a liar. Things change in a minute." He frowns. "I'm worried about Tabitha. I don't know how she's going to handle all of this. She relied on Grant for so many things."

"I know, me too."

I study my husband. Some men get better looking as they age, and he is one of them. As a teenager he was kind of gangly and cute, but now, he is downright hot. Tonight, he's fresh shaved from the funeral, but usually he has a bit of scruff which I like. Since we moved to Little Beak, Zach has upgraded himself. Expensive, sleek haircuts, well-cut suits; Grant got him doing his workout at the gym and the confidence I see in him with his career makes him so attractive. I've noticed all those things before, but when something like a death occurs, you start to really look around at the people close to you and appreciate them.

I lean over and kiss him and again, deeper this time. I sit my drink down, take off my cotton shorts and undies, straddling him, my knees sinking into the sofa as I press my body against his.

"Talia," he whispers, quickly putting his drink down and pulling me even closer to him.

He shrugs his shorts off fast and we give each other exactly what we need. A release.

"I love you so much," I say, kissing him again before I move off him. I put my clothes back on and pick up my drink again, satisfied.

"I love you," he says, doing the same. We sit in quiet for a few minutes, just enjoying the moment.

"I'm really worried about Tabitha handling everything too. Do you think she'll be able to do it?" I ask.

He takes a drink of scotch and pops a couple pretzels in his mouth. "I don't know, but she kind of has to."

"I'm glad Mom and Dad are staying with her this week," I remark.

"Yeah, that's good."

After the funeral I got our parents settled in the apartment over Tabitha's garage. They can stay in the house, there is plenty of room, but they always insist on using the apartment. They say they like their privacy. I think it's because Dad snores so loud, and Mom is worried he will wake everyone up. Either way, they are in the apartment.

Tomorrow is Friday. We closed the bakery for the week. I will go in on Tuesday, but I doubt Tabitha will be in next week, probably longer, understandably so. I'll handle everything until she's ready to come back. I want her to take all the time she needs for herself and Cole. I'm so grateful we hired Claire; the extra help will be needed over the next few weeks.

"Are you going over tomorrow?" Zach asks.

"Yes, actually, we are," I say to him. "I told Mom I'd go to the grocery store, and we'd make brunch at Tabitha's house for everyone. You're helping me."

"Am I?" he laughs.

"You sure are," I reply. "So, let's finish our drinks and go to bed. You have a lot of grocery shopping to do tomorrow."

"I'd do anything with you." He squeezes my hand.

Zach and I carry the groceries inside Tabitha's house, where my parents are already making coffee, and a strawberry smoothie for Cole, who perches on a wide stool at the kitchen island.

"Good morning," we greet everyone.

"Grandma made me a smoothie!" Cole exclaims, eyes bright. The beauty of youth's innocence.

"Oh, yum!" I say.

"Looks good, buddy," Zach replies, placing the groceries on the counter.

Mom whispers to me: "I moved all the flowers over to the dining room table. They were just everywhere in here. I thought it best to clear out the kitchen. We'll just eat in here."

"Yeah, the kitchen is best for brunch anyway," I agree.

Even though the obituary said donation to cancer research in lieu of flowers, many flowers still arrive, along with baked goods and casseroles—thoughtfulness I'm sure Tabitha appreciates.

"Hey, Dad," I say, giving him a hug.

"Talia, my favorite girl." He smiles. He always says that to both of us.

Zach already has bacon cooking, and the smell makes my stomach grumble. I put out the bowl of fresh cut fruit from Whole Foods so we can snack until the food is ready. I grab a chunk of cantaloupe and pop it in my mouth.

"I'll make eggs and hash browns," Mom says, getting out a frying pan.

"And I'll do pancakes and French toast. Chocolate chip or blueberry, Cole?" Dad asks.

"Chocolate chip!"

"OK, then."

I put the orange juice and pineapple orange, my personal favorite, into the Sub-Zero refrigerator. I retrieve a mug from the cabinet and pour a cup of coffee. They seem to have brunch covered.

"I'm going to check on Tabitha," I say, leaving the room.

I walk up the open staircase and turn right to go to her bedroom. The door is open. Tabitha sits at her vanity table, brushing her long blonde hair.

"Hey," I say, walking inside the room.

She turns. "Hey." She puts down the brush and picks up a small pot of lip balm, slathering it on her lips.

"How are you?" I ask.

"Tired of people asking how I am," she retorts. "I mean, really, how do you think I am?"

"They mean well."

I walk over to her and give her a hug. She reciprocates. Tears well in her eyes.

"I'm not okay," she says, gazing at me. She looks vulnerable, younger than our thirty-two years. I worry about her. I don't know if she can handle everything.

"Of course you're not," I say softly. "Losing Grant is a huge shock. You loved him. He loved you. You're not going to be okay for a while, and that's okay."

"He was cheating on me," she sniffs.

I hug her again. "I know, but he did love you. You know that. And he loved Cole. Try to remember the good things. You two had so many good things in your life and good memories."

She nods. "Yes, that's true."

She grabs the brush again and runs it through her already silky hair a few times. "I'm not sure what I'm supposed to do now."

I pick up the lip balm and dab some on my lips. "You take it one day at a time."

"I know." She stands up, pulling back the curtain on the window next to the vanity table. "Oh, look who's walking up the driveway."

I join her at the window. Side by side we stand watching Anne walk slowly up Tabitha's dark paved driveway, carrying a large covered glass casserole dish. She stops for a moment, staring at some bright purple plants in one of the many island flowerbeds, then, as if she senses our presence, looks up directly at us. She waves. We wave back.

"I know she had something to do with Grant's death, his murder," Tabitha growls. "I want to rip her head off. There's something wrong with her."

"I know, you're right. Something is off about her." I hesitate to tell her about what Anne said about the pictures, and the fact she wasn't home Saturday or Sunday morning; who knows what time she got home on Sunday. She could have been the driver that killed Grant. Fact is, Tabitha's hanging on by a thread, I can sense it, and this information will have her spinning out of control and I don't want her losing her mind doing something she couldn't come back from... like killing Anne. Is Tabitha capable of doing something of that nature?

We stare at Anne. Tabitha takes a deep breath. "I saw her with Grant a couple days before he was murdered."

My gaze goes to her. "What do you mean?"

"I was in the city for an appointment and wanted to

surprise him at work. I saw them talking outside his office building."

I ponder this for a moment. I'm not sure if Anne and Grant even met one another, at least not that I am aware of. "Maybe they met, and we didn't know it. We are neighbors. They may have just been saying hello."

Tabitha's face twists in anger. "My God, be on my side for once! It didn't look casual. The conversation appeared more in depth. It was weird."

Her anger surprises me. "I am on your side, Tabitha."

She lets out a huff. Then silence.

"Did they know you saw them?" I ask, breaking the silence.

"No, I just watched. They spoke and then he went inside the building. She stood outside the building, just staring. I know she's hiding something."

I nod. My stomach turns. I think she's right. "Yes, something is wrong. None of this makes sense."

Anne continues to the front door, casserole dish in hand, like Tabitha would ever eat anything she made.

Tabitha turns to me. "Finally, my sister believes me. Don't worry, I won't flip out on your new friend like I want to. I'm going to be subtle, to find out what she wants."

"Really?" Honestly, her words catch me by surprise. I don't think Tabitha knows the meaning of the word subtle. "She's not my friend," I mutter.

"Hmm..." Tabitha gives one more look in the vanity mirror and turns toward the door. "Let's go say hello to our dear friend Anne."

Anne is already in the kitchen. Mom gave her a cup of coffee and is trying to talk her into staying for some food, but she refuses.

"No, thank you, but I must go." She directs her gaze at

Tabitha. "I just wanted to drop off this lasagna and pay my condolences."

"Thank you, Anne." Tabitha strides over to her. "I do appreciate the thought. I see you met our parents."

"Oh, yes," Mom says. "But, Anne, I didn't get your last name."

"Graveley," she replies.

"Anne Graveley," Mom repeats. "Why do I know that name?"

"Anne's a writer, a mystery author," I explain. "Maybe you read some of her books."

"Are you serious? Did you write *The Secret*? I read that book a couple months ago and loved it!" Mom exclaims. "You know, when I first saw you something seemed so familiar about you. I think your smile. I must have been thinking about your picture on the book."

"Oh, well, thank you. I'm glad you enjoyed my book." Anne smiles warmly.

"It's strange when you meet someone for the first time and there is some sort of connection, a familiarity," Mom continues. "I loved the setting of *The Secret*, upstate NY, it reminded me of our little town."

"Good to hear," Anne says. She takes a sip of coffee.

"Anne, thank you so much for coming and the lasagna," Tabitha says to her, curtly, clearly wanting her out of the house.

"Of course, you're welcome." Anne sits her cup on the cluttered kitchen island. She turns to Mom. "It was wonderful to meet you. I understand about feeling that kind of connection." Anne reaches out and gives our mom a brief hug, which my mom reciprocates.

"So good to meet you, Anne," Mom says.

Anne turns and waves to the rest of us. Are those unshed tears in her eyes? She walks out the front door.

Tabitha shoots me a look. What the hell was that? I shrug.

Who is Anne Graveley?

The purple microfiber cloth I use for dusting reaches its limit for dirt, so I swap it for a new blue one. I hadn't realized it was so long since I'd dusted. Not exactly on my current list of priorities.

Zach has told me for years to hire a housekeeper and it partially appealed to me. It's not like I love dusting and cleaning the bathrooms, but I don't like the idea of someone else in my house, cleaning my stuff. I'm perfectly able, so why not do it myself?

I pick up a silver frame of Zach and myself on our wedding day, polishing it until it shines. Almost ten years ago. Hard to believe that many years have passed since that beautiful day. Finished wiping the frame, I place it back on the mantle.

I lay the dusting cloth down and go over to fill up my coffee mug. It's Monday morning, just a few days after Grant's funeral and the brunch at Tabitha's house. I am almost finished cleaning, but my mind strays from the menial task, still running over Anne's interaction with Mom at Tabitha's house and my sister's reaction.

Tabitha called me last night to talk about it again. Why did Anne hug Mom? Why did she look like she was going to cry? Admittedly, the whole situation was strange. I chose to let it go. Everyone gets overemotional at times, it happens, but Tabitha kept hounding me asking those same questions, like I knew the answers.

Our parents are staying the week, which is good. Tabitha needs them around. Zach and I are going over there for dinner tonight. Mom's making her famous fried chicken and baked macaroni and cheese. I sip my coffee and put a piece of wheat bread into the toaster. Tabitha's reaction to Anne still surprises me. She held herself back, so unlike her. I wonder how long until she explodes. I'll give it a week.

The toast pops and I smear butter on it. I take a bite and another sip of coffee. Grant has been filtering in and out of my thoughts the last few days. Life is so unpredictable. What you know as your reality can change in an instant. There's Grant, going to a doughnut shop to get his son some of his favorite treats, and he is killed. He couldn't have avoided it. He was healthy, strong, intelligent, yet his destiny was predetermined. He had no warning to change the direction of events.

I will always remember the trip Zach and I took with Grant and Tabitha to Niagara Falls. We stayed at the Hilton on the Canadian side and had great views of the Falls. It was a spur of the moment trip, before they had Cole and before we moved to Little Beak. The four of us spending a silly, fun weekend together, going on the *Maid of the Mist* boat and all the touristy activities. Grant was from high society, a phrase my mother always used, but he was not snooty, arrogant, yes sometimes, but I always enjoyed his company, and we had many good memories together as a family. I miss him very much.

What if, somehow, he knew, sensed, what was in his future? If one says destiny is predetermined but another factor intervened, could that cause another direction to open without negative results?

I finish my coffee and put the cup into the sink. Such deep thoughts for a Monday morning.

TWENTY-EIGHT

TALIA

I frost the last vanilla crème cupcake, add orange sprinkles and cute candy pumpkins to the top of each one. Today is Halloween and tonight trick or treat night. Several businesses on Main Street are hosting trick or treat parties, and almost all ordered cupcakes for their event. The evangelical church in town is throwing a party as an alternative to trick or treating, and they placed a large cupcake order. Luckily, Tabitha came in very early today to bake, her first day back at the bakery since Grant's death. It works out well since Mom and Dad can take Cole to school this morning. After she was finished, she went to the gym. I'll be closing the shop today, then going home to get in my costume to join everyone for trick or treating. Hopefully, Zach will make it home from work early enough to come with us. My cheerleader costume needs his football player costume. Couple costumes are the cutest.

Only two weeks have passed since Grant's death and Tabitha was going to skip Halloween altogether. Trick or treating is a family affair and, losing Grant so recently, she thought doing the tradition would be too much for Cole, under-standably. But Cole's friend begged him to go with him, dressed as ninjas, as they had planned. It had seemed odd to all of us to be going out, but if Cole wanted to do it, we would try to enjoy the night for his sake. Our parents were originally going to stay only a week, but now are planning to leave next week. Tabitha is happy to have the extra support around, but three weeks is the limit for houseguests, even if they are your parents. Grief still consumes her, as it would anyone in that situation, but I think she wants to try things on her own. Her and Cole figuring out this new life they now have to live.

I've been decorating cupcakes all morning and my right hand aches. This vanilla crème is my last batch. I glance at the clock. Eleven thirty. The morning has flown by fast.

The front door of the shop jingles. Claire's at the counter, so I don't pay it any mind until the door to the back room opens and Tabitha flies in, her hair disarrayed in a messy ponytail, her eyes wild, directed at me.

"I punched Kim," she says.

"What?" I wipe my hands on the apron and walk toward her. "Are you serious?"

She nods. "Yep, she was at the gym, said she missed it and her new gym wasn't the same. She said we should support each other now that Grant's dead. As if I want anything to do with her!"

"Then you punched her," I say. Wow. She is losing her mind.

"Yes, I think I gave her a black eye. I grabbed my bag and left." Tabitha sighs. "I guess it was stupid, but I couldn't help myself."

"Very stupid," I agree. "I wonder if she'll press charges."

Tabitha paces around the room. "Do you think she will? No, I don't think so. She wants us to be best friends, like fucking sister wives or something."

"OK." I take off my apron and hang it on a wall peg. Tabitha is on the edge, overwhelmed by all the intense recent events. I want to help her in whatever way I can, even if she doesn't want me to. She always thought she could take care of everything. "Let's go down to the café and get some lunch. Claire can take care of everything for a bit."

Tabitha nods. We walk out front, tell Claire we are going out to lunch, and start down Main Street to the café, just a short five-minute walk. The gloomy day is fitting for a Halloween day. Heavy clouds hanging above, and rain threatening all day to fall, yet none has, yet. I hope none will for trick or treating with Cole tonight. He is dressing up as a ninja and seemed happy for the distraction from everything that is going on in his life.

Dry leaves crinkle underfoot as we make our way to the crowded café. The waitress shows us to a table in the back by a large window facing the street. A large hanging basket of ivy dominates the center of the window, spilling its long, shiny green leaves. We place our orders.

"I don't know, Talia," says Tabitha. "The affair with Kim I can deal with; it seems so unimportant now that he's gone, and I know we would have got past it. But a baby... ugh."

"You have enough to deal with now," I say. I take a pause. "Do you think Kim could have been the hit-and-run driver? Grant broke it off with her and it sounds like she was devastated."

"I've thought of it," Tabitha says, taking a sip of water. "But stealing a car, running him over, getting away. It's too complicated for her. I don't think she could plan something like that."

"I think you're right," I agree. "She's not diabolical and all of that would take a diabolical mind."

"Anne, on the other hand..." Tabitha raises her eyebrows.

"I know, right? What was that weirdness with Mom last week?" I ask. "I mean, I understand getting emotional, we all have those times, but I've been thinking about it and how strange it felt. But maybe we are overreacting, and it was one of those times when emotions take over without any reason."

"Everything about her is strange," Tabitha says. "I am certain she had something to do with the hit and run."

"Have you heard anything new from the police?"

"No, they are waiting for more video from the expressway; hopefully some of the person without the face mask."

"Good, I hope they get some so you can get answers," I reply.

"I need answers." She pauses as our grilled chicken salads arrive. "I also need a new toilet handle."

"Why?"

"Last night, in the master bedroom, I flushed the toilet and it kept running, it would not stop, and the toilet handle doesn't do anything. I don't know what is wrong with it, so I shut the valve off. I guess I'll have to call a plumber."

"What about Brian?" I ask. Brian is the handyman they usually use for jobs around the house.

"Oh, he's not available," she says quickly.

"Um, Zach can fix that for you," I say. "Same thing happened to ours last year. Can you wait until tomorrow night? Tonight will be busy."

"Yeah, that would be great."

She stabs her romaine and another jab to the cut-up chicken. "So, are you and Zach still having sex?"

I almost choke on the piece of chicken in my mouth. I swallow and answer. "Yes, we are. Why are you asking me?"

"Because you want a baby but you're not pregnant yet," she says, matter-of-factly.

"It's a lot more complicated than that, but we have plenty of sex," I retort. "You are unreal, Tabitha."

She never fails to surprise me. I am here supporting her, and she throws in that barb to make me feel inadequate. Classic

Tabitha. She isn't that naïve, but she wants to remind me she still has something I do not, and maybe never will: a child. She always needs to be top dog in whatever we do in life and me coming in a lowly second place.

"Hey, I didn't mean to offend you," she says. "I was just asking a question."

"No, you were purposely being rude, like you always are," I say. "Look, I know things are hard right now. Awful. But don't take it out on me."

I signal to the waitress and ask for a takeout box for my remaining salad.

"Why are you getting so mad at me?" Tabitha asks. "I just asked you a question."

"You know it is a sensitive subject for me, but you keep going with the smart little comments. I don't want to hear them. Zach and I will be over at your house at six to go trick or treating. I'll see you then."

I take my food box, pay my bill, and leave the café.

Main Street in Little Beak swarms with superheroes, witches, princesses, and scary creatures. Dim streetlights and creepy jack-o-lanterns in every store window, including Little Beak Sweets, add to the eerie, blackened night. Cole and his friend, Tyler, stride ahead of us, both dressed as cool ninjas, holding pumpkin-decorated bags already heavy with assorted candy. Tabitha, aka Catwoman, Mom and Dad, donning pumpkin and ghost sweatshirts—that is as far as they go to wearing a costume —walk behind them, along with Tyler's parents. Zach and I, cheerleader and football star, bring up the rear.

I'm still mad at Tabitha, although not as angry as this afternoon, just a slow simmer now. I'll probably be over it by tomorrow, but tonight I really do not want to speak to her.

We walk into Dan's bookstore, Little Beak Books. Little ghosts and goblins are already helping themselves to cupcakes and cookies he has set up in the center of the store at a large oval table covered by a skeleton tablecloth and a large glowing skull in the middle of the table.

"Oh, cool!" Cole and his friend exclaim, running ahead to stare at the skull.

We walk at a slower pace through the well-organized bookstore. Only open for about a year, Dan's store is well stocked, but also allows the customers to linger, with comfortable leather chairs and a couple wide coffee tables, a bright and cheerful children's area painted in sunshine yellow, a coffee center in the back of the store, and large, stylish, cozy rugs in warm reds and golds adorn the dark hardwood floors. He has created a space where everyone feels welcome and comfortable to shop and hang out for a bit.

Zach joins the boys to inspect the skull. I snag a Snickers bar from one of the candy bowls and turn to a large book display to the left of the Halloween table: *Anne Graveley, New York Times Best Selling Author.* Dan has all her books here, both in paperback and hardcover. I pick up the glossy hardcover of the book she gave me, *The Secret*, and make a mental note to start reading it this week.

"Here's another." Tabitha puts a Snickers bar in my hand. "And I'm sorry."

I accept the candy. "Thanks."

"Girls, these cupcakes are divine!" Mom says. "I never had the salted pretzel before."

"New flavor, Mom," I say.

"You'll never get better than your chocolate with peanut butter icing," says Dad.

"You always say that," Tabitha laughs.

"Because it's true!" Dad exclaims.

"Let's keep going!" Cole says, walking up to us, white frosting on his upper lip. Tabitha wipes it off. We follow him out the door to the next location. That candy bag better be strong.

We walk along in the crisp night air. We see a few friends and customers among the ghoulish dressed crowd, all in search of more calorie-laden sweets. We reach the ice cream shop. Covering the store windows are spider webs and large black spiders hanging from them. Only a few people milling inside as we go to the door. As soon as Zach opens it, Cole begins to howl.

"I don't want to go in there!" he cries.

Tabitha is by his side. "Oh, we don't have to go in there, Cole."

Tears stream down his sweet face. "Dad got me ice cream from there. Peanut butter swirl. And chocolate for me."

Tabitha hugs him and signals for us to give them some space. We move a bit down the sidewalk to give them privacy. Cole hasn't said much about Grant's death. He is probably still in shock. This is a good step in expressing his feelings about everything. Grant's death is a huge shock to all of us and I'm sure unbelievably overwhelming for a six-year-old.

A few minutes later we pile into Tabitha's SUV and drive the short distance home. The car ride is somber, all of us in our own thoughts. As we drive, many of the houses still have trick or treaters traveling to their doors. Bright orange jack-o-lanterns and spooky ghosts decorating the porches. The next house is dark as the night. Not one single light shines at Anne's house.

"I guess the writer isn't giving out candy," remarks Tabitha, edgily.

"So, this is Anne's house," Mom says. "What a nice girl and so talented."

Tabitha and I share a look. Talented at writing and what else? Murder?

THIRTY

TABITHA

A stack of dry-cleaning sits on the edge of our bed, my bed. Grant's suits, pristine in plastic wrap, have resided there for almost two weeks. I didn't want to move them. I haven't slept in our bed either; instead I slept in one of the guest rooms or sometimes in Cole's room, if he has nightmares.

Today is the day I will put the suits away. I haven't decided if I will hang them in his closet or donate them. I open the door to his closet, a walk-in like mine, but smaller, and step inside. A dim scent of his cologne still lingers in the small space. A blue pullover is slung over one of the shelves. I pick it up and hold it up to my nose, inhaling the scent of Grant, my husband. I remember when he wore it, just a few weeks ago, at the harvest festival. Oh, I loved him. I sob.

Memories flood me. Our young love filled me with such excitement and hope for our future. He was the only one I wanted, and he gave me the life and stability I had craved. Grant knew how important stability was to me, especially when we had a family. When Talia and I were young, our father was an alcoholic and would disappear for days at a time. He didn't only disappear from home, but work, too. He lost many jobs and he and Mom would argue all the time. Mom supported us in those early years and worked hard. I have so much respect for her, but I vowed I would never live a life like that, wondering how I'd support my children. Thankfully, Dad got help when we were ten years old and started living a sober life. Our family grew closer and more stable, but I never forgot how it felt at eight years old and Mom, Talia and I would eat scrambled eggs for dinner and not know if Dad was coming home that night. Right in the beginning of the relationship, Grant promised he'd always take care of me, and he did, but I wasn't enough for him, but I guess that was my struggle. I am thankful for the time we had together.

I put the pullover on over my tank top and survey the neatly arranged closet. Nobody tells you when someone passes away it's those quiet, small moments that impact you the most. I realize in these moments that I'll never feel his arms around me, or his lips against mine. We'll never share a laugh or just enjoy time spent together. I ache for Cole, losing his father, and he has been so quiet about everything. We talked about Grant last night and he understands that his father is gone, but he's always with us in memories and spirit. Healing happens over a period of time, but small steps are taken every day. We have an appointment with a child psychologist, who specializes in grief counseling, next week. I hope it helps him.

The police are still investigating some leads. There are a few eyewitnesses to the hit and run as well as camera footage from the doughnut shop. Eventually we'll get some answers to Grant's murder, but coping with his loss from our lives will be a much longer process.

THIRTY-ONE

TALIA

I stock the iced coffees in the cooler and am about to go to the back room to get the juices to fill the bottom row when the bell jingles as a customer enters Little Beak Sweets. I have barely turned away from the refrigerated case before Kim is in my face.

"You better tell your crazy ass sister to calm down," she yells at me.

I stare at her. Her right eye is slightly black and blue.

"Kim," I hiss at her, guiding her to the back room and trying to avoid Claire's interested gaze. "Be quiet."

"Quiet? You don't think the whole town knows by now?"

I maneuver her to the back and close the door, although I'm certain Claire is listening on the other side. Kim's probably right, the whole town surely knows about the affair, the baby, and the punch.

"I know you're upset," I say in a low voice. "I get that. Tabitha was wrong to hit you. I'm sorry about that."

Kim sighs. "Everything is so awful right now. How could Grant be... dead?"

Tears well in her eyes.

"I know." I hug her awkwardly. Hugging the woman who is

pregnant with my sister's deceased husband's child is odd. Something from a soap opera, not real life.

"I only wanted to be friends with Tabitha. My baby will be part of her family," says Kim. She pulls away from me, her perfectly made-up face now streaked with tears. Her long, glossy hair hangs midway down her back. She wears jeans with a soft floral sweatshirt and slip-on sneakers. She's younger than us, probably twenty-five, but standing there she doesn't look older than seventeen. She has made some bad choices, but I feel sympathetic toward her.

"I don't think she sees it that way," I say.

She nods. I don't know what else to say to her. I certainly couldn't change Tabitha's mind. She will lose her mind if she walks in on us having this conversation.

"Give her time," I suggest. I point to a tray of salted caramel cupcakes. "Would a cupcake help?"

"No." She gives me a weak smile. "But I'll take one."

I load the last dishes into the dishwasher and click it on. A quick wipe of the kitchen counter and everything is clean and in its place. Zach comes downstairs in a gray T-shirt and old faded jeans.

"I'm going to Home Depot and then over to Tabitha's," he says. He walks over to me, and we kiss. "I don't know what time I'll be back."

"Don't worry about it. I'm going to have some wine and finally read that book Anne gave me," I reply. "What does Tabitha have you doing tonight? Something with her closet?"

"Yeah, the closet and clean drains in the bathroom. She has a list," he says.

"Hopefully this is the last handyman visit you make, at least for a while," I say. "Thank you for doing these things for her. I know it's a hassle, and I'm not sure why Brian isn't available to do these jobs. He's been their handyman for years."

"I don't mind. It's simple things." He pulls on a sweatshirt. "Have fun reading your book. I'll see you later."

"Bye."

I watch him walk out the door. This is the second Friday Tabitha has requested his services. I have a sinking feeling her list might be never ending.

I pour a tall glass of pinot grigio, turn on the gas fireplace, click on the reading lamp, grab a cozy chenille blanket, and snuggle in with Anne's book, *The Secret*.

It hooks me midway through the second chapter. Her writing is fast paced, and the story draws me in. I take a long sip of wine. I can see why Mom mentioned the setting reminded her of our small town in Finger Lakes; I have the same feeling.

I gaze at the fireplace, always enjoying the warm homey feeling it gives to the room. I turn the book over, wanting to look at the photograph on the back cover Mom mentioned when she met Anne. No photograph, just a book description and a blurb stating, *New York Times Bestselling Author*. Hmm... strange. I page through the book; I've read other authors that have a photograph toward the back of the book. Nothing. A brief biography, nothing new there, a list of book club discussion questions and an excerpt from an upcoming book. No photograph. How would Anne seem familiar to Mom if she never saw her? Could she have seen her on TV?

I grab my phone from the coffee table and type in Anne's name. Her books come up and her literary agent, her publisher, the brief biography, one photograph of her in a black turtleneck sweater, a couple links to podcasts she's been on, but no TV shows or videos of any sort. I zoom in on the photograph. Maybe Mom saw this picture?

She looks much younger in the photo. Maybe around twenty-four or twenty-five. I don't know how old Anne is, but I assume around our age. I stare at the picture for a few minutes until I realize what I'm staring at. Her eyes. The palest of blue, not the vivid green eyes she has now.

She must wear contacts.

I remember when Tabitha and I met her officially for the first time, she wore glasses and had green eyes. If she wears contacts, though, why would she need to wear glasses? I've seen her wear the tortoise-shell-style glasses on other occasions, too.

My gaze goes back to the fireplace. Calming in its simplicity and warmth. Despite its warmth, a coldness comes over me, creeping up my spine, snaking a way over my skin, creating goosebumps and uneasiness throughout my body.

I shiver.

I pull the blanket close to me, still staring at the fire. The coldness will not go away. I consider forgoing the wine and making myself a cup of hot tea, but I don't want to get up. I close my eyes, snuggling deeper into the blanket, trying to generate more heat. Long frosty fingers creep up my spine and around my shoulders.

I shiver again.

My gaze lifts from the fireplace over to the glass French doors leading outside to the patio.

Anne stands on the other side.

Watching me.

THIRTY-TWO

TALIA

My phone drops from my hands onto the expensive patterned wool carpet. I grab it and shove it into my pocket, hoping when I look back at the door, Anne will be gone. Maybe I'm only imagining her standing there. I'm thinking about her. Maybe I nodded off and only thought I saw her standing at my patio door. I slowly look again.

She still stands there.

Is she there or am I imagining her? How much wine did I drink?

She waves.

I wave back. I guess she's real.

I reluctantly walk over to the door. My stomach churns so much I think I may throw up on her. If she is a figment of my imagination, little good that will do.

The door creaks open.

Anne steps inside.

We stare at each other for a moment until she breaks the silence.

"Sorry to bother you, but I wondered if you had a tape

measure? I'm ordering a new cabinet for my office and want to see if it will fit in the space I want to put it," she says.

"Oh, um, I think Zach has the tape measure with him," I say. "He's over at Tabitha's doing a little work around the house."

"OK, I had one when I first moved in, but I have no clue where it is now."

"It's easy to misplace things," I reply.

"Sure is," she agrees.

"Actually, I was thinking about you. Wondering if you want to join me for yoga sometime, since you couldn't make it last time."

Anne nods. "Sure."

I look at her. "What happened last time when you canceled? I'm not sure if you told me." I want to find out where she went for those few days. The same time period Grant was murdered.

She sighs. "Oh, my friend had unexpected surgery and I went into the city for a few days to help her."

"Oh," I say. "I hope she's doing well."

"She is, thank you for asking." She looks over into the family room. "Looks like you're having a relaxing evening, fire, wine, is that a book?"

I grin. "Actually, it's your book."

Anne raises her eyebrows. "What do you think?"

"I'm only on the second chapter, but I'm hooked," I say. "Care to join me for a glass of wine?"

Keep your friends close, keep your enemies closer. The only way I can find out Anne's secrets is to get closer to her.

"I'd love to." She smiles, her green eyes sparkling.

Green eyes.

Not blue.

I retrieve another wine glass from the cabinet, fill her glass and take the wine bottle over to the sofa with us.

Anne takes a sip. "This is nice. I love sitting by a fire."

"Same, so calming." I laugh. "The wine helps too."

"It certainly does," she agrees. "So, how's Tabitha doing with everything?"

"So-so, she's getting through it."

"It takes time. I had a hard spell after my mom died two years ago."

"Oh, I'm sorry," I say. "I'm sure that was difficult."

"And Zach is helping at her house a lot?" she asks, an edge creeping into her voice.

"Yeah, last week she had an issue with the toilet. This week something with her closet and bathroom drains," I reply.

"Hmm..." Anne says.

"What?"

"I'd wonder why she suddenly needs your husband at her house every week, but that's just me." She takes another sip of wine. "I am the suspicious type."

I was thinking the same thing earlier. Grant and Tabitha had Brian, a handyman that did odd jobs around the house when they needed done. The first time when she mentioned the toilet issue, I brought up Brian, but she said he wasn't available. Why isn't he available anymore? Why does Tabitha need Zach there? Does she just want the company?

"The thought crossed my mind," I admit, but I'm not sure why I have told Anne. She has a questionable balance of terrifying me and appealing to my sensibility.

"Maybe you should join him next time, or do a surprise visit?" she suggests.

I take a long guzzle of wine. My face flushes from the alcohol and Anne's suggestions. Do I have something to worry about between Tabitha and Zach? It seems like a crazy thought, one brought up by a person I don't know well, or even trust. Why does this thought resonate so deeply in me? Is it something I always suspected but never wanted to know the truth?

"You know, Anne, maybe I should," I say. I pick up the bottle. "More wine?"

I wake up at twelve thirty. The fire is still on, the wine bottle is empty, and Anne is gone. I'm finally warm.

Was she ever here? I look at her book lying on the coffee table. Did I imagine her visit? Only one wine glass sits on the table. I grab it to place in the sink. Another wine glass sits inside the deep kitchen sink.

She was here.

I walk over to the French doors, lock them, and pull all the blinds. My head aches. I travel upstairs to get a Tylenol and go to bed. I'm certain Zach is already asleep. I'm surprised he didn't wake me up to go to bed with him when he got home.

He isn't sleeping. He isn't even in our bed.

What the hell? He's still at Tabitha's?

I pull my cell out of my pocket and call him. Right to voicemail. I text him.

> Where are you??

Nothing.

I call Tabitha. Voicemail.

Anger surges in me. I call him again.

"Hello?" he answers groggily.

"What are you doing?" I demand.

"What? Oh, shit, I must have fallen asleep," he mumbles. His voice clears. "We were watching a movie with Cole. I'll be home in a couple minutes."

I hang up the phone. Anne may be right. Maybe I should have a suspicious mind, too.

· · ·

Zach paces around the living room, the vein on his forehead bulging with anger. "You had her here! In *our* house? What is wrong with you?"

"What's wrong with me? What the hell is wrong with you?" I yell. "Falling asleep at my sister's house and yelling at me for having a friend over?"

"She's not a friend!" he screams. "You asked me to go over to your sister's house after I worked all day! Now you're mad because I fell asleep watching a movie! Fuck!"

He picks up Anne's book and hurls it across the room, hitting a framed photograph of us at Niagara Falls that sits on the end table. The frame flies off the table and smashes into pieces on the hardwood floor. Small glass shards scattering everywhere.

I glare at him. He stills, staring at the smashed frame. Anxiety and fear rise inside me. I have witnessed him in this state on other occasions, but his intensity tonight scares me more than any other incident. I go to the pantry to retrieve the broom and dustpan to clean up the mess. When I return, only moments later, he calms a bit, takes the items, and cleans up the broken glass.

I go to bed.

THIRTY-THREE

TALIA

I look into the large oval mirror above the sink in our small bathroom in the bakery. I dig my hand into my purse and retrieve the lip balm lying on the bottom. I detest lipstick, Tabitha and I both do; we always go for balm, sometimes gloss.

I slather it on my dry lips and pause for a moment, studying my reflection in the mirror. I recently had my hair done, now a glossy honey-blonde mane, and I wore makeup today, so I look pretty good. My hazel eyes, always browner than green, give warmth to my face, and the diamond studs I wear, an anniversary gift from Zach a couple years ago, give me just enough sparkle. Not bad.

I smooth over my red dress worn over black leggings and high black leather boots. So happy it is boot season once again. I love wearing boots, and I house a lot in my closet to wear.

You'd think I am going out on a date rather than shopping with Anne and then out to dinner. I invited her. I want to talk to her and ask her directly about the Hamptons, and she said she needed a new dress for an event in Manhattan next week, so tonight is the night.

Tabitha and Cole are at a family event at Grant's parents'

penthouse. They are leaving early this afternoon and won't be back until Saturday around lunchtime. Zach has a work function tonight; he'll be home very late. Perfect for a little shopping and dinner with Anne.

Zach is driving me crazy after his behavior the other night. He was fine the next morning. He apologized, but this whole week he has seemed different to me. I'm glad to be free of him tonight. Tabitha has been cool to me too. Her behavior has me wondering how much Zach's anger had to do with her. How often do the two of them talk?

I hope tonight will just be about new dresses and a nice dinner. I'm sick of dealing with my life at this point. I canceled our appointment at the IVF doctor this week. Zach is so unpredictable. Do I really want to have a baby with him? Lately, he has been giving me serious doubts.

The front door jingles.

"I'll be right there," I call, putting the lip balm back into my purse.

Anne stands in the shop. She wears black jeans, short black boots and a soft pink cashmere sweater.

"Ready to shop?" she asks.

"Yes!" I reply, walking out with her, turning off the lights and locking the door behind us. "Let's go to Lillian's Boutique first," I suggest. "I think they have the best selection of dresses. Are you thinking short or long?"

"I'm not sure, probably longer. I'll know when I see it," says Anne. "Something conservative. I don't like flashing everything around." She laughs.

"I know what you mean." I smile as we make our way to the store.

A successful shopping trip makes us both happy. Anne found a stunning dark green Chanel dress, form fitting but in a classy, conservative style. I found a new sweater set in a deep purple; Tabitha will be thrilled. We each found new boots, chocolate brown for Anne, dark maroon for me. Shopping is always so pleasurable when you find treasures.

"Do you want to eat at Suzy's?" I ask. Suzy's is a restaurant known for their seafood and steaks. One of Zach and my favorites. One problem though. "Damn, I completely forgot to make reservations. We're never going to get a table on a Friday night without one."

"No big deal," says Anne. "Let's get a pizza. We can go back to my house and watch a movie. It's only seven o'clock."

"Yeah, let's do that," I say. "Zach probably won't be home until after midnight."

We get a pizza from Antonio's and go to Anne's house. The last time I was here, Tabitha and I had broken in. OK, technically, I had a key, so we just walked in, uninvited.

We sit on an older-style sofa with recliners built into both ends, quite comfortable. We watch a British movie about a detective in the English countryside. Not something I'd normally choose, but I liked it. Very interesting movie.

We down the pizza and merlot in record time. All that shopping must have stirred our appetites. Our conversation moves from clothes shopping and movies to how Tabitha is doing dealing with Grant's death to vacations. I see an opportunity to ask a needed question.

"Have you ever been to the Hamptons?" I ask.

Anne looks thoughtful for a moment. "No, I don't think so. Oh, now wait, a couple years ago I was there for a party with a friend. Have you?"

I nod. "Yes."

Silence stretches between us for a few moments. What is she thinking about?

"I don't want to be nosy," Anne says. "But what time did Zach get home last Friday?"

I shoot her a look. *You are being nosy.* "Late."

"I thought so. It was eleven when I left," she says.

"He was watching a movie with Cole and fell asleep."

"Yeah." Anne nods. "And he and Tabitha are both in the city tonight?"

"Anne, why do you always do this?"

"Do what?"

"Bring things up that I don't want to talk about?"

"I told you. I have a suspicious mind."

"Yes, that's true. Do you think I should have a suspicious mind, too?"

"Yes, I do," Anne says, her lips curving into a smile. "Suspicious minds force secrets to be revealed."

"I don't have any secrets," I say.

Anne takes another drink and laughs. "We all have secrets."

THIRTY-FOUR

TALIA

I pull on my short black wool coat over my new purple sweater set, don black gloves to keep my hands warm and grab my purse, to walk over to Tabitha's house. I would have rather lain down on the sofa and taken a nap, not only because I'm tired, but I want to keep an eye on Zach, as well.

Now the second week in November, winter has crept in with its icy grip. Snow is in the forecast tomorrow. Nothing big, a few flurries but flurries mean the start of an East Coast winter. Cold, snowy weather is okay if I'm curled up by a warm fire, but I can't say it is my favorite season.

Tabitha and Cole returned this morning around eleven. Cole has a basketball game at the elementary school at two. I'm riding along with them. Zach stayed home. He'd only gotten home after two in the morning and had a headache and didn't feel great. I'll deal with him later.

I travel up her driveway and enter through the side door to the laundry room. A few more steps and I'm in the kitchen where Cole is eating string cheese and Tabitha is on her phone. She lays it face down on the counter when I enter.

"Oh, there you are!" she exclaims. "I was just going to text you."

"Am I late?"

"No, Cole's just anxious to go," she explains.

"OK." I smile at Cole. "Finish your snack and we'll go."

My gaze diverts to something shiny lying on the kitchen island. Something familiar. Where did that come from?

"I'll get my coat," Tabitha says, leaving the room.

Cole contentedly eats his string cheese, staring at the TV on the far wall. I snatch the shiny item and shove it in my pocket.

"How was the city?" I ask Tabitha when she reenters the room.

"Oh, fun. The family dinner was good, and I did some shopping," she says vaguely.

"I stayed at Grandma and Grandpa's apartment. It's a penthouse," Cole says. "All by myself."

"Well, not all by yourself." Tabitha smiles. "Your grandparents were there."

"But Mommy stayed in a hotel. Grandpa and I made chocolate sundaes with cherries on top. I put three cherries on top of mine," he says, his attention diverted by the TV again.

"Really?" I look at her. An uneasiness builds inside me. She is hiding something.

"I needed a little alone time," she says. "Grant's parents didn't mind, so it worked out."

"Oh," I reply.

Tabitha moves closer to me, opening my coat. "Did you get another sweater set? What is wrong with you?"

"I'm beginning to wonder," I reply, pulling away from her and closing my coat.

After the game we sit in Tabitha's kitchen drinking hot tea with honey. Cole goes upstairs to take a shower and play video games. Tabitha leans against the counter and sips her tea. She studies me, sitting quietly at the kitchen island.

"What did you do this weekend?" she asks. "Besides buying that awful sweater set?"

"I went shopping with Anne, then we got a pizza and watched a movie at her house," I say, bracing for her response. I know she will flip out. She always does when I spend any time with someone other than her. The only person she doesn't get jealous of is Zach.

"You did what?" she bellows. She gives me an incredulous look. "What?"

"We had a nice time," I say.

Tabitha is silent. Strange behavior for her. "I'm very shocked by this," she says in a controlled voice.

"Well, it was just shopping and a pizza," I reply.

Tabitha sits her mug of tea down. "You know, I haven't seen Anne in a long time, probably not since before Halloween. I haven't even noticed any lights on in her house."

I laugh. "OK, I saw her last Friday and yesterday. She's still around."

"I'm sure she is," Tabitha says, wearing a Cheshire cat grin.

Before I go home, I walk over to Anne's house. I ring the doorbell. No answer. The curtains are drawn on all the windows and no lights appear to be on. I notice a few copies of the *Little Beak Gazette*, a free weekly paper, piled by her front door. Were they there on Friday when I was over? I don't know because we went into the house through the back door.

I shrug and walk to our house. I put my hands into the sweater pocket, feeling the shiny object I'd snatched from Tabitha's kitchen counter. I stare at the sleek silver pen. It has the same hotel name as the one I found a couple months earlier on my patio.

. . .

I chop vegetables for the soup, carrots, potatoes, onions, and add them to the savory broth cooking on the stove. Zach comes downstairs and opens the refrigerator, taking out a soda.

"Smells good. What are you making?" he asks.

"Vegetable soup," I reply.

"Should I get the panini press out? Paninis would be good with soup."

"OK, sure," I agree.

He rummages around in the bottom cabinet and retrieves the panini press. He sits it on the counter. "OK, now I'll be ready to make them when the soup is done. When do you think? About an hour?"

"Yeah, it's better when the soup sits a bit," I reply.

"Do you want to go to the movies tonight?" he asks.

"Sure, what's on?"

"I don't know, but I just thought it would be fun."

I point to my laptop on the kitchen island. "Look at my laptop to see what's playing tonight."

"OK." He walks over to the laptop and leans on the counter typing on the keyboard.

I turn away to stir the soup cooking on the stove. A few moments later, the laptop slams shut and Zach stomps over to the French doors, looking out into the yard.

"What's wrong?" I ask, turning away from the stove.

"We're not going to the movies!" he yells, pacing.

I stare at him, confused. "Why? What's wrong?" I repeat.

"We're just not going," he screams, grabbing his car keys from the counter. "I have to go."

"Where?" I continue to stare at him. Fear trickles through me, as it always does when he has his outbursts. This one truly came out of nowhere.

He ignores me and walks out to the garage.

What the hell?

One minute he's fine and the next he's flipping out. What did he see on my laptop? I open it up. Two browser windows open on the screen. The website of the hotel written on the silver pen that I found at the party and at Tabitha's house. The other is Anne's author photo.

THIRTY-FIVE

TALIA

I place the last cupcakes, vanilla latte, into the large pink box. Four dozen for a promotion they are running at the bank where Zach used to work before his promotion to the main headquarters in the city. Zach is attending and taking the cupcakes.

I lift one box and then another, sitting them on the counter. Tabitha comes out from the back, wiping her hands on the pink apron she's wearing, which is splattered with flour.

"Trouble with the mixer?" I ask.

"A bit," she says. She walks over to the cooler and takes out an orange juice. She opens it and takes a drink. "Are those Zach's cupcakes?"

"Yeah, he should be here soon." As I say the words, he walks inside the shop with Dan from the bookstore.

"Good morning, ladies!" he says. He walks over to me, giving me a kiss.

"Hello, ladies!" Dan greets as well.

I retrieve Dan's two dozen cupcakes and place them on the counter. He is one of our best customers.

"Thanks, Talia," he says. "I am really craving a salted caramel cupcake today, so one of them will be mine."

"You deserve it, Dan," I say. "How's business going? Your bookstore is beautiful. I just love it."

"Things are very steady. I have my book club regulars and quite a bit of foot traffic. The children's programs are flourishing too. I'm very happy with the business," he says.

"Cole loves your new comic book section," Tabitha states.

"That's been pretty popular," he remarks. "I want to do another book signing with your neighbor, Anne. I've had several people request signed copies of her books and the last one was such a success. Unfortunately, I haven't had any luck reaching her."

"You have her cell phone number?"

"Yeah, and it's a correct number. I've talked to her before, but I've been trying to reach her since a little after Halloween, but she never returns my calls. I hope she's okay."

"How strange," I say. "Well, I saw her the last two Fridays. We went shopping last Friday; we should have popped into your store."

Zach drops the box of cupcakes he holds onto the floor. It lands with a heavy thud.

"Oh no!" I yelp.

Zach slowly picks the box up and places it on the counter. He looks at Tabitha oddly before turning to me.

"You went shopping with Anne on Friday?" he asks.

"Yeah, I thought I told you." I lift the box lid. A few cupcakes have their frosting squished, but otherwise okay.

"Where did you go?" he asks, his gaze intense on me. Tabitha now joins him across the counter from me.

"We did some shopping at Lillian's and got a pizza, then went to her house and watched a movie."

"You went to her house?" his voice growls.

I stare at him. His tone angering me. "Yeah, why are you acting so weird?"

"He probably didn't realize you two were becoming good

friends," Tabitha chimes in. "Your behavior has been weird lately."

"OK, so if you see Anne, have her call me," Dan says awkwardly. He takes his cupcake box and leaves, obviously happy to exit the suddenly uncomfortable environment.

"My behavior is *not* weird. You two are being weird." I shove the box to Zach. "These are fine. Just have the employees eat the ones with the flat frosting."

A customer enters the shop. Zach nods and gives Tabitha a questioning look.

What the hell is going on here?

Why are they acting so odd about Anne? We went shopping and ate a pizza together, big deal. I don't think she had anything to do with Grant's murder. What motive would she have had? And Tabitha better mind her own damn business.

I wait on the customer. Zach turns and walks out of the shop, the bell jingling his exit.

He leaves without saying goodbye. Asshole.

The heavy gloom of the day makes the view from Dr. Bales's office less interesting than normal. Today I stretch out on the cream sofa with a seafoam green pillow under my head. Damn the cliché.

"Have you been sleeping, Talia?" Dr. Bales asks, her dark-framed glasses halfway down her nose. "Are the pills helping?"

"At first they were, but I think I need something stronger." My throat catches. "Especially with everything lately."

"Sure, no problem. Maybe something for your anxiety, too?"

"Yes." I nod.

"Tell me, what is happening?"

"Zach's been so irrational lately." I tell her about the laptop incident. "First, he's so inconsistent with making decisions. I know you and I have discussed this before. Sometimes I feel like

I tell you the same thing every week when I come in to see you. He gets so angry about small things that have me wondering what he's even upset about."

"Except the IVF process that we've been discussing every week." Dr. Bales looks at me, her brown eyes full of compassion. "That is a big issue and to toy with your feelings about the subject is hurtful to you and serious. He's not treating you as an equal partner or respecting your feelings."

I know she's right. Zach is not treating me as an equal partner, and now that I think about it, has he ever? My life always revolves around his whims, and Tabitha's. Why have I allowed myself to go along with it for so many years? What about me? I am a person who deserves respect, but I get none from either of them.

I nod. "That's true."

"What do you think Zach saw on the laptop that angered him so much?" Dr. Bales asks, typing on her laptop.

"There were two browser windows I had open. One was a website for a hotel. The other an author profile picture of Anne."

"Anne, the woman who lives next door to you?"

"Yes."

"Would Zach have any connection to the hotel, or think it was strange you would be looking at it?"

"I don't think so."

"That leaves the photo of Anne." Dr. Bales pauses. "Why would this enrage him?"

"Tabitha doesn't like her," I say. "He always thinks I should be on my sister's side. Maybe that's why?"

She clears her throat. "Maybe you should consider why your husband takes your sister's side over you."

I fall silent. I have already wondered about that.

THIRTY-SIX

TALIA

I put the groceries into the refrigerator. Apples, orange juice, eggs, cheese, butter, yogurt all go into their respective places. My mind isn't on grocery items, however. My thoughts all center on Anne.

I haven't seen her since we went shopping and watched a movie last week. Nothing. Her house looks like a tomb, day after day, no lights on, curtains completely closed. Those weekly papers still stacking up by the door, a new one arriving this week. I texted her a couple days ago, but no response. If she came to Little Beak to write, why isn't she here half the time? And where did she go?

Zach's and Tabitha's behavior has been nothing short of strange, especially whenever I bring up the subject of Anne, like mentioning our shopping trip. My thoughts about Anne are in turmoil. I'm suspicious of her one day and really enjoy spending time with her the next. She's like a puzzle to me that I can't quite figure out. I like her, I consider her a friend, yet I don't completely trust her. I feel as if she is keeping something from me, but I am worried about her. Tabitha fills Zach with her suspicions of Anne, and I continue to be the third wheel. I wish

Anne was around because she is the only one I talk to about them, other than Dr. Bales. She seems to sense I need to talk to someone about it, and that something continues to be amiss with them.

I close the refrigerator door and go to put a couple boxes of crackers and coffee in the pantry. Tabitha has been remarking about not seeing Anne lately too. She brought up the idea of using the Edwards' house key to check out Anne's house again. I told her my suspicions that Anne may have cameras set up inside her house, but she still wanted to do it. I consider it. If something is wrong, maybe I can help; if not, she already knows I'm a nosy person since I snooped around earlier. Maybe she wants me to snoop if she's in trouble. I don't want to go alone, though: What if there is a body in the house now? I should just stay away and mind my own business, but I know that isn't going to happen.

I put the items on the pantry shelf, then walk into the back-yard. I go back to the hole in the bushes in the back. I peer through the hole and scan Anne's backyard. Dusk just arrived and the yard is dim and shadowy. Normally people will have a light on at this time. I look at our house, where the kitchen lights are shining brightly through the windows. Anne's house is completely dark. I consider for a moment, then decide to walk over. I won't go into the house, just walk around her yard for a bit.

I round the bushes at the side of our house and walk across her side yard, over to the concrete back porch. My vision is dim—I should have brought a flashlight—but nothing appears unusual. The patio table has four cushioned chairs tucked neatly under its lip. A lounge chair sits in a different place than usual, closer to the porch. The house remains dark and quiet. I slide up to the sliding glass door at the center of the porch and try pulling it open. Locked. I continue over to the window over the kitchen sink and peer inside, craning my neck to see if I can see any lights inside, possibly in the basement. Nothing but blackness, except a small nightlight plugged in on the opposite wall at the window. I want to explore more. My phone beeps. I pull it out of my pocket. Tabitha.

> Why are you snooping around Anne's yard?

A little laugh escapes me. I walk back to my yard. Tabitha is standing by the opening in the bushes, my usual spying spot.

"Why don't we just go inside if you're so worried about her?" she says, hands on her hips.

"Will you go with me?" I ask.

"Of course. Cole is at a sleepover tonight, so I'm free all night."

"Well, I'm not spending the night there," I say. "Just a quick in and out to make sure everything is okay. Come over here around eleven. I don't want Zach to know we're spying on her."

I sit in the patio chair waiting for Tabitha's arrival. Zach fell asleep shortly after ten and I've been monitoring Anne's house all night: no activity, everything still dark and still. My obsession is starting to get on my own nerves, but I feel compelled to go inside.

Tabitha arrives ten minutes after eleven. She walks over and sits in the patio chair opposite me.

"Why are we doing this?" she asks.

"I'm worried about her. I haven't seen her for days and she doesn't answer my texts."

Tabitha glares at me and taps her fingers on the table. "Let's go and get this over with. Do you have the key?"

"Yes." I hold it up. "And a flashlight for each of us. I don't think we should turn many lights on in case she is in the house."

"Why? What's the difference if we use flashlights or turn on lights?"

"It's what Nancy Drew would do," I tell her, a laugh escaping me.

"You're a nut." Tabitha laughs.

"Probably, although we are kind of crazy." I laugh.

"No doubt," Tabitha agrees. "We'll go through the garage like last time, check to see if her car is there, if not, we will go inside and put on minimal lights and have a quick look around."

"Don't forget about her cat," I remind her.

"Yes."

We leave the patio and hasten over to Anne's house, letting ourselves in through the back door in the garage. Anne's car is gone so we continue into the house. I put the key into the door-knob and turn. We walk inside the kitchen and stand in the dark for a few minutes, just listening. Silence. Tabitha flicks on the light by the door and the Tiffany-style light over the kitchen table turns on.

Everything is neat and tidy in the kitchen. No dishes in the sink, clean counters, kitchen table with a bright yellow bowl of ripening fruit, some already rotting. Despite the aging fruit, the house smells fresh, like lemon, as if a cleaning has recently been done.

We continue through the house, where nothing appears amiss, everything seemingly in order. The house remains quiet, eerily so, as if it is listening to us move about instead of us listening for its sounds. A coldness lingers in the structure, not necessarily cold, but a thin, wispy whoosh of cold that came and left just as fast. I don't know if it is a draft from a window, or a heating issue, but it spooks me. We creep upstairs, using our flashlights, creating shadows on the walls of the stairway. We reach the top, still silence surrounding us. A large floral painting hangs at the top of the stairs. Candle sconces mounted on either side of the picture.

"She must have taken Gilbert with her," I whisper to my sister.

"Or he's hiding," she replies, holding her flashlight in my face. "Who cares?"

We tiptoe down the hall to the master bedroom, giving the other bedrooms a quick look over, nothing unusual, and pause at the bathroom in the main hall. A few drops of water pool on the white tile floor with blue diamond shapes scattered throughout and a slight heat emanates from the room, perhaps steam, perhaps from a recent shower taken by someone? The shower curtain is pushed wide open. Tabitha shines her light around the room and opens the closet, nothing. We take a deep breath and continue. Finally, we approach the main bedroom at the end of the hall.

The door is closed. Tabitha turns the knob and slowly opens it. I stand close behind her and we shuffle inside. Moonlight streams in through a large window in the front of the generous sized room, its heavy brocade curtains open wide—different from the tightly closed curtains downstairs. A sleek vanity table sits to the side, a patterned wingback chair with a sweater draped over it, a large modern-look dresser, a door, partially opened to the adjoining bathroom, a faint light emerging from the space, and in the center against the opposite wall of the window, a large, probably king-sized bed covered in a thick, cream-colored bedspread and pillow shams matching the bedspread, neatly made without one crinkle in the covers.

Lying atop the bed, flush on the creamy, soft surface, just below where the pillows are lined up in a perfect arrangement, something unexpected.

Something not quite right.

I raise my eyebrows at Tabitha, and she narrows her eyes, motioning to move closer to the bed so we can give it a closer inspection.

We shimmy closer, practically glued together at this point,

and stand at the edge of the large bed with a soft, light gray cushioned headboard and stare at what lies on the neatly made bed.

A Halloween costume. A cheerleader costume in bright red and white. Not the store variety, but homemade, and certainly not new. The costume is stained—dark stains, all over it—and torn in certain areas. It lies on the bed, the moonlight shining directly on it as if it is on display. Peculiar it isn't an adult-sized costume.

It is sized for a teenager.

"What the hell was that?" I ask, barely able to breathe after we tear out of Anne's house upon seeing the strange costume lying on her bed. We are back in my backyard, catching our breath.

"I am never going back into that house," Tabitha swears. "Never."

"Why would she have an old Halloween costume lying there like that? It looked so weird. What is the point of a dirty old costume lying there? Is it some sort of message? Maybe a message to us for snooping around her house?" Hysteria is taking me over now. I just want answers to what is going on.

"No clue, but I'm going home." Tabitha stomps off toward her house.

I sit in my quiet backyard. Tabitha isn't going to help me. Zach isn't going to help me. I know what each of them thinks about Anne. I'm on my own to find out what exactly is going on with Anne. I hear Tabitha's door slam shut at her house. I can't get the image of the costume out of my mind, along with a slinking inkling of familiarity that I have seen it somewhere before. And where is Anne? Something else is nagging at me too. I'm certain all the curtains in her house were closed when I looked at it earlier this evening. Certain. I've been checking every day. If the curtains in the bedroom window, which is at the front of the house, had been open, I'd have noticed.

I leave my patio chair and walk over to the front of Anne's house. I stand just a bit away from my driveway. The house is still and quiet, dark, and creepy to me now. I stare up at the master bedroom window, where Tabitha and I were only moments earlier.

The curtains are still open, but the right curtain appears to flutter, as if someone moved away from the window.

I gasp and run back to my house, locking the door behind me and closing all the shades.

I have barely slept tonight, despite the new prescription for sleeping pills I had filled earlier in the week. I wonder if they are too strong for me because I have felt so unbalanced lately; but if they are too strong for me, wouldn't I still be able to sleep through the night?

I stumble out of bed to use the bathroom and get a drink of water. I splash water on my face and try to clear my mind. Thoughts of the curtain flutter still linger in my mind. Did the curtain move or was it my imagination? Was someone in the house when we were snooping around? Was it Anne? Why would she be hiding in her own house? My thoughts jumble.

I lift my robe from the hook in the bathroom, intending to go downstairs for some juice. Zach is still sleeping deeply in our bed; he has never had trouble sleeping like I do. I pad down the quiet hallway, pausing at the top of the stairs, staring at the bedroom at the far end of the hall, the door open.

This is the bedroom facing Anne's house. A strong desire to look out the window and survey the surroundings envelops me. I walk toward the open door. I enter the room, neatly decorated in a tasteful midnight blue and creamy white furniture. The curtains are closed. I open them slowly.

The moon shines only half of its brightness tonight, partially obscured by clouds. I look down at Anne's yard, dark and still. Everything appears still, the entire world asleep, except for me. My gaze travels to Anne's dark house, up to the second-floor window of one of her guest bedrooms.

This window is not dark.

A dim light is on inside the room. The curtains pulled wide open. The faint light is enough to illuminate the figure standing in the center of the window.

A girl stands at the window. A girl wearing a stained, tattered cheerleader's costume. A girl who stares through the window directly at me.

Panic seizes me and I drop onto the floor, shaking. I pull my knees close to me and rock. Who is that? What's going on inside Anne's house? I want to look again, but terror still swells inside me.

I sit on the floor for a long time. Finally, I creep up to the window, only my eyes peeking over the sill.

The window is dark now, curtains pulled closed.

Was the girl ever really there?

THIRTY-SEVEN

TALIA

My dining room table is set with our finest Royal Albert bone china, burnt orange fabric napkins, pristine tall Waterford glassware, ready for chilled drinks, all atop a warm butternut-colored tapestry tablecloth. The buffet at the side also boasts a butternut runner which hosts an array of desserts, including a pumpkin cake with cream cheese icing—the special at the bakery this week—pumpkin pie, pecan pie and assorted cupcakes. Elegant crystal candlesticks stand flickering on both the table and buffet, lending a warm, cozy ambiance to the room.

The turkey in the oven smells divine along with the potato filling. Mom is originally from Pennsylvania and potato filling is a traditional dish for Thanksgiving dinner that she always made, and we continue the tradition. Sweet potatoes, fully baked, give a sweet aroma, soon ready for cinnamon, brown sugar and butter to be added to them.

There will be seven of us for Thanksgiving dinner. Zach's parents are going to his brother's house in New Jersey. I invited Anne to join us, much to Zach's displeasure. I explained her parents are dead and she is an only child. She was planning on spending the holiday alone. He didn't seem to care, but that's his problem. Anne returned the day after Tabitha and I had found the odd costume in her bedroom. She said she'd been away visiting friends and had taken Gilbert with her. I didn't mention how we broke into her house again and she didn't say anything, or act uncomfortable around me, so I let it go. I can't explain my ever-changing feelings about Anne. On one hand, I'm certain she's hiding something from us. Is it sinister, or just odd? Then on the other side, I enjoy spending time with her and really like her. I sense a special friendship between us; a comfortableness exists when we spend time together, as if we've known each other for years. I only wish I could find out what she is hiding from me. Maybe I should talk to Dr. Bales about my conflicting feelings at my next session.

I don't know if she is telling me the truth or if she was hiding in the house that night we went over. Someone was in that house that night though, I'm certain of it. The curtain fluttered, didn't it? I don't have any answers about the girl I saw in the window. Was she real? I don't think so. I wonder if I had been sleepwalking and having a nightmare. I woke up that morning in the upstairs hallway—I never even made it to my bed.

I still think about the cheerleader costume. I know I have seen it, or something similar, somewhere. Did I see a similar costume when we were trick or treating? I doubt it: This was an older, homemade costume. Why did it have so much damage? Stains, tears, it was severely damaged, not a result of a regular trick or treat night. Was someone killed in this costume? A young girl? The girl I thought I saw in the window. Is she the victim? My mind is sick with worry. I need to get to know Anne better and figure out this mystery. Why would she display something like that on her bed?

I did place cards this year, placing Anne between me and Mom; hopefully, I thought, this would placate Zach and

Tabitha. They would be at the opposite end of the table. I walk back to the kitchen to retrieve the breadbasket. Zach stands at the stove, stirring the gravy, and cooking the carrots.

"How's it going?" I ask.

"Gravy's just about done. Where's the gravy boat?"

"Right here." I point to the pumpkin-style gravy boat on the kitchen island.

"OK, thanks." He smiles at me.

I return the smile, grab the breadbasket, and go back to the dining room. Things have been strained between me and Zach, as well as me and Tabitha. The closeness of the two of them is unnerving and I don't know if I trust either of them. Tabitha refuses to talk about our findings in Anne's bedroom, flat out refuses, which shocks me. She is nosier than me, and I would have thought she'd be all over this and want to explore Anne's house more, which I would refuse, but she acts like it didn't even happen. More mystery. Tabitha's and Zach's obsession with my friendship with Anne continues to grow and bond the two of them even more.

Against me.

I don't know how I became the third wheel between my husband and my sister. Today is Thanksgiving and I'll put that aside to be thankful. Hopefully, today will mark a fresh start for all of us.

The doorbell rings.

I go to the door to let my parents inside. Just as I'm about to close it, I spy Tabitha and Cole walking up the driveway and Anne walking out her front door.

"Wow, good timing, everyone," I say. "I only have to open the door once."

Everyone inside, I close the door as they hang up their winter coats.

"Everything looks and smells so good!" Mom exclaims.

"It sure does!" Dad agrees, looking at the place cards. "These are fancy."

I laugh. "Have a seat. Everything is ready. I'm going to help Zach in the kitchen."

"So nice to see you again, Anne," Mom says. Her voice gets fainter as I enter the kitchen.

Dinner is a success, right down to the homemade cranberry sauce. Now we all sit with full bellies, slowly eating our choice of dessert—pecan pie for me—and sipping on coffee, hot chocolate for Cole.

"I'm stuffed," Tabitha says, poking at her piece of cake. "I don't think I can eat any more."

"Oh, I can," Dad says. "If you don't want it, send it over here."

Tabitha pushes her plate over, and he proceeds to eat it.

"How's the writing going, Anne?" Zach asks, a surprising edge in his voice.

I look at him; my eyebrows rise.

He ignores me.

"Really good," Anne says. She lays down her fork, only crumbs left of her pumpkin pie. "I finished the first novel; now I've begun the second. Everything is flowing so quickly with these books. It's as if they are writing themselves. I've been so focused on writing I haven't been giving time to anything else. Dan from the bookstore keeps leaving messages about doing another book signing and I've yet to get back to him."

Anne perplexes me. She hasn't been home for days, yet she says she has been writing. I realize she could write from anywhere, but she said she was visiting friends. What is she trying to hide from me?

"Well, cheers to you." Zach holds up his wine glass. My parents take this as a genuine congratulation and hold their glasses up. I hear Zach's sarcastic tone, but join them as well, and Tabitha does the same.

"Cheers to Anne's writing!" Mom says enthusiastically. We clink glasses and drink.

"Thank you," Anne says, shooting me a look, undoubtedly picking up on Zach's tone.

"I can't believe we'll be getting some snow this week. Of course, more up our way," Dad says, in between bites of cake. "Remember when you girls couldn't wait to go sledding every year? You would pester us every day about when there would be enough snow."

"Oh, yeah, and we'd go sledding at Zach's house," I say.

"You had that huge hill behind your house," Tabitha says. "We had so much fun sledding down that hill. Walking up wasn't so fun though."

Zach laughs. "I remember when the two of you talked me into pulling you up the hill in the sled. Never again."

"Such good memories." Mom turns to Anne. "Where did you grow up, Anne?"

"Ithaca," she says.

"Wow, I didn't know that," Mom replies. "That's only half an hour from us in Watkins Glen. Isn't it a small world?"

Anne lifts her wine glass and takes a sip. "It is indeed."

It's the next evening, and I flick off the TV and stare at the fireplace, mesmerized by the warm embers. Zach and I had a quiet dinner, and he soon went to bed, claiming his new position at the bank was exhausting him. I had thought about continuing to read Anne's book but wasn't in the mood. Instead, I watched a movie about a bunch of teenagers in high school. Now memories flood my mind.

A Homecoming Dance when we were sixteen. Tabitha had a date with the quarterback of the football team, and the two of them were crowned Homecoming King and Queen. Zach and I went as friends. The dance was okay; a couple girls snuck peach wine coolers in, and we drank them in the school bathroom, giggling that we were *so* drunk.

Tabitha and her date, I don't remember his name, had a big fight, and he ended up leaving the dance with Jennifer Beck, a sophomore, and Tabitha screamed at them at their departure. Zach ran to her side and the two of them disappeared into the parking lot.

I had a huge crush on Zach for the last year or so and was so excited to go to the dance with him. I got a new spaghetti strap short black dress and I felt like a princess going to the ball with her prince; but my prince didn't care about me, at that time: he only had eyes for the queen.

I watched him follow her out the door and anger surged in me. He was my date. He was here with me, but he was really with her. Nothing new.

I followed them into the crowded parking lot to the back row where Zach parked his blue Chevy Camaro that he'd refurbished over the last two years. A light rain fell, and I hid from the rain behind a tree to the side of the parking lot, affording me a clear view of Zach's car.

Tabitha was pacing by the passenger side, the rain no concern to her, now running down her new slinky dark purple dress. The shiny silver crown still sat atop her head. She was crying and yelling; Zach was trying to talk to her, calm her down. I knew, because I'd seen him do the same many times in the past; but she wasn't listening.

He put his hands on either side of her, leaning her against the passenger door of the car, and kissed her for a long time. She didn't push him away; she returned the kiss. A romantic kiss in the rain. My heart sank. I didn't have a chance with Zach if Tabitha wanted him.

I was the third wheel.

The next day everything was normal. I never mentioned the kiss and neither did they. They weren't dating, we were all just friends, as always.

Even after Zach and I got together, years later, I sometimes thought of the kiss in the rain that night. The passion between them.

Could that be reignited?

Am I the third wheel again?

THIRTY-EIGHT

TABITHA

I pour the bowl of chocolate chips into the mixing bowl. I walk to the refrigerator to retrieve the eggs when the door in the shop jingles. I wipe my hands on the apron. Talia and Claire have already left for the day, so I'm the only one here.

I go out to the front of the cupcake shop, where Anne sits at the table by the window, drinking an iced coffee from the cooler. She wears faded jeans, a black hoodie, and sneakers.

"Tabitha," she simply says, holding my gaze.

"Anne," I reply, walking over to the table, ignoring the chair, preferring to remain standing.

We continue staring at each other. I glance at the clock. Ten minutes until the shop closes. Why is she here?

I glare at her. I don't have time for her games. "You know, I was wondering something."

"Sure." Anne doesn't seem to blink.

"That day in Antonio's, why didn't you say anything to me, or tell Talia I was there?"

"I don't remember," Anne says, appearing thoughtful.

"Sure," I say. I don't know why I thought I'd get a straight answer from her. The woman is a conundrum, and I don't trust her for a second. "Oh, I have your lasagna dish in the back. Talia was going to drop it off at your house, but she forgot it. I'll be right back."

I travel to the back room and retrieve the dish. Pausing at the doorway, I watch Anne. She still sits at the table, now staring out the window. Images of the old cheerleader costume Talia and I saw in her bedroom a few weeks ago filter through my mind. Why did she save that old, tattered costume? Why is she here and how can I get rid of her? For good.

I stride out and place the dish on the table. "OK, I'm closing soon, so if you want something else you need to ask now."

"Just some cupcakes, please," says Anne. "A dozen."

"Having some friends over?" I ask.

"Something like that," she replies, holding up the iced coffee. "Don't forget this too."

"I don't forget anything," I retort, going to the cupcake case and opening a pink box for her baked goods.

I lock the front door of Little Beak Sweets after cleaning up the back room. I stayed later tonight making that last batch of chocolate chip cupcakes. Talia needs to decorate them tomorrow morning for the elementary school basketball tournament in the afternoon. Thoughts of Anne fill my mind. I wonder who the friends are that she would be sharing the cupcakes with. Funny, I have never seen Anne with anyone, other than Talia. In fact, the two of them seem closer than ever, despite Grant's death, the weird pictures and costume we found in her house.

It's now December, over a month since Grant's funeral. Cole and I have fallen into a routine, and I think we are both coping the best we can due to the circumstances. Cole is a brave little boy, and I'm immensely proud of him. He goes to the child psychologist once a week, and talking to her has helped him work through the grief of losing his father. I feel like we are on the right path now, or at least can see the sign pointing toward it.

The door now locked, I pause for a moment before turning away, staring at the coffee shop across the street: Little Beak Coffee. Anne sits at a table by the front window, eating a sandwich and undoubtedly drinking a coffee. How much caffeine does that woman consume in a day? She just had an iced coffee here. Her hair is different than when she was in the shop, pulled back by a clip, away from her face. She chews a piece of sandwich, swallows, and then turns to stare directly at me.

I don't shy away. I'll stare that bitch down if that's what she wants. She doesn't scare me. Our gazes meet for, what feels like, an eternity. I still have trouble believing it's her even though Zach showed me the picture on the laptop. And I am not about to let her know I am now privy to her secret.

Then she cocks her head to the left.

A cold chill enters my body, racing up my spine.

Yes, it is her.

Why is she here? To settle old debts?

Danielle.

She's supposed to be dead.

I continue to hold the stare with Anne, as she calls herself now, trying to push away the uncomfortable thoughts crowding my mind. She finally looks away, focusing again on her sandwich. I turn to gather my things and head home. I hadn't thought of Danielle in years, not until Zach raced over to my house that night.

I watched her die.

Or so I thought.

THIRTY-NINE

TALIA

Zach and I enter the Grand Ballroom located in the Marriott in Lower Manhattan. He is devastatingly handsome in his black tux, and I'm looking good, too, in my gold, beaded Ralph Lauren tulle gown, borrowed from Tabitha. The room is bathed in warm blue and white hues, crisp white tablecloths on round tables, white chairs, silver and gold centerpieces on each table filled with shiny ornaments in an array of blue colors, and four small blue candles flicker around the centerpieces. White twinkle lights adorn the various Christmas trees in the room. Only two weeks until Christmas, hard to believe.

Tonight is the annual bank Christmas party. I wasn't in the mood to go to a party, being social, and putting on the mask of happiness, but it's important to Zach that I attend, so here I am, doing things for Zach. Well, not exactly for Zach, I only want to keep up appearances at this point, if I'm being honest.

We find our seats toward the front of the room, near the podium. Zach goes to get us some drinks, and I watch the people filtering in. Some I know, some I do not. Being out in a different environment around different people feels good to me. I know some answers to Anne's secrets—not all, I'm sure. I don't think she is a bad person or hurts other people. I can't see that in her. Tabitha and Zach are wrong about her. I don't know what to think about Tabitha and Zach anymore.

My thoughts drift over the past two weeks. Quiet would be the best word to describe them. Everything has been very calm since Thanksgiving, and I'm thankful for the lack of drama in my life. Zach is consumed with work, but back to his fun, charming self, at times, and we even did some Christmas shopping together last weekend and had a nice dinner out. The weirdness between us has faded, like always, at least somewhat. I know the unstableness will return, as it always does with Zach, but I enjoy the calm periods. The information I recently learned about him is something I am still processing.

Tabitha has fallen into a steady schedule of Cole's basketball games and volunteering at his school. She's been going out to lunch with some of the PTA ladies and is sometimes too busy to meet up with me. I think it's good she has other friends. She has even started coming into the bakery early. She is quieter too, almost subdued. My guess is it's because the police still don't have any real answers about Grant's hit and run and who was driving the car. Tabitha has even invited me and Anne over for a Christmas tea this coming Monday. I am surprised, but it sounds fun to me. I'm hoping she realizes she is wrong about Anne.

I have spoken to Anne a couple times, and she came over for coffee at my house last week. She is busy writing her books, so she's keeping a low profile. She has a book signing at the bookstore scheduled for the next week though. We had an intense conversation last week and I'm still floored by her revelations.

I wave to Jim, Zach's boss, and his wife, Lindsay, when I see them enter the room. They wave back and walk my way, reaching me just as Zach comes back with our drinks.

"Hey, guys," Zach says, handing me a margarita.

"Hello, Zach," Lindsay says, looking stunning in a form-fitting red gown and bold diamond earrings. "Are you getting out on the dance floor tonight?"

"Not me," Jim replies. "Not with these knees."

"Well, then it will just be us." Lindsay laughs.

"I think I can manage a dance or two," Zach replies, giving Lindsay a wink.

"Please join us," I say. "I think the hors d'oeuvres are coming around."

"Shrimp canapes for me." Lindsay turns to Jim and points to my margarita. "I'll take one of those."

"I'm on it," he says. He and Zach walk back to the bar.

"Zach is loving his new position," I remark to Lindsay. "I'm so happy for him."

"Of course, I'm sure you are."

"All of those late nights and weekend conferences, especially the last few months, have been worth it," I reply, tasting my margarita.

"Conferences?" Lindsay asks.

"Yeah, the weekend conferences. There's been three since summer."

"I don't know about that. Jim hasn't attended any weekend conferences. Maybe it was some kind of training Zach had to attend for the new position."

"Oh," I say, now draining my drink. Odd. Zach mentioned Jim attending the last one. He said they'd shared a hotel room.

"It's so pretty in here," Lindsay remarks, quickly changing the subject. "Very Christmassy."

I nod. Anger rises inside me thinking about how Zach has lied to me. Where was he all those weekends when he was supposedly at work conferences? And who was he with? Anne's warning about Zach and Tabitha plays in my mind. But he was talking about and going to these imaginary conferences before Grant was killed. And my sister would never betray me like that, but something isn't right. There has to be a reason he made up these work events to be away from me.

There has to be someone else.

Who?

Lindsay is still talking but I have no idea what she is saying. I excuse myself and leave the room to use the bathroom. Only moments ago, I walked into the ballroom feeling beautiful and excited to be here. Now I feel like a firecracker ready to pop and explode over everything.

I walk down the hall to the restroom, my heels clicking on the tile floor. A young man dressed in a smart dark gray suit passes me, then stops.

"Mrs. Conner?"

I turn. I don't know him, but with a friendly smile on his face, he obviously knows me.

"Yes?" I say with a question.

"Xander, the concierge?" The young man continues to smile, though it's dimming slightly. He seems genuinely confused, as if we've spoken many times and it's odd for me not to remember him.

"Sure," I play along. "You've arranged so many things for us."

He laughs. "Well, you and Mr. Conner are one of my favorite couples that stay at the hotel. I appreciate your generous tips. I know I've told you that before, but I really mean it."

I laugh, my anger boiling at this point, mixing with sharp hurt. Tears on the verge of exploding from me. "Of course. Gosh, I wonder how many times Mr. Conner and I *have* stayed here?"

Xander replies. "Quite a few, almost too many to count over the last year or so. Well, it's good to see you. I'm done for the weekend, but hope you have a great time tonight."

"Thank you, Xander," I murmur as he continues down the hall.

I feel sick. I don't want to believe it, but who else could be staying with Zach at this hotel? Who else could he mistake me for? It all clicks into place as I realize it's the same hotel as the pens I found on my patio and on Tabitha's kitchen counter. There's only one answer to my question: someone who looks exactly like me.

My twin.

Now the question is, what am I going to do about it?

FORTY

TALIA

Monday

Two days later, snow swirls around us as we walk through the tree line on Tabitha's property and across her driveway. A few wet flakes land on my nose, and I wipe them away. Only a light snow but enough to be a nuisance. I pull my warm red hat farther down my ears.

"We should have driven over," Anne says, her dark curly hair covered in snowflakes, a snow-white knit hat atop her head.

"Probably," I agree. "But we're here now." I smile at her, still thinking about everything we've been sharing over the past week. It's amazing that she and I are here together.

We trudge up the driveway. The snow doesn't bother me. I like snow. It's beautiful. Christmassy, pure, I have no problem with snow. I do have a problem with going to my sister's house for Christmas tea when all signs point to her sleeping with my husband.

Somehow, I managed to get through the dinner on Saturday night. We stayed overnight at the hotel. I told Zach I was sick and to stay away from me. I wasn't pretending. I am sick.

Of him.

Things were silent on Sunday between us and now, Monday, Anne and I are going to Christmas tea at Tabitha's house. Nothing spreads Christmas cheer like a tea with the sister who is screwing your husband.

We knock on the front door, decorated with a fresh balsam fir wreath, a bright red ribbon on top. I brush a few snowflakes from my coat. Tabitha opens the door. She is wearing a dark blue sweatshirt and leggings. Not very festive.

"Hello!" she greets us in a sing-song voice. "So glad you could come. Let's head into the dining room. Hang your coats over there."

A dark green tablecloth hangs on the dining room table. A three-tiered serving tray sits in the middle filled with cupcakes, macaroons, and assorted candies. White plates with delicate holly edging sit at three place settings. A chocolate raspberry cupcake sits on each plate.

A thump comes from upstairs.

"What was that?" I ask.

Tabitha appears unconcerned. "Oh, probably the wind."

Anne and I share a glance.

Tabitha directs her gaze at me, my winter coat still on. "Take your coat off, Talia."

I look at her and Anne, who hung her coat up on the row of hooks in the foyer, pointed out by Tabitha.

"Sure," I say casually, unbuttoning my long gray wool coat. I toss it onto a side chair.

"Does it look familiar?" I ask her. Adrenaline pulses through me, enjoying my choice of outfit, infuriating my sister.

Tabitha glares at me, then turns to Anne. She's pulsating with fury and I feel a sick joy at what is about to happen. "Did you put her up to this?" Tabitha demands. "I know who you really are, you know."

"Glad to see me again, Tabitha?" Anne returns the stare.

I flounce the red and white pleated skirt of the cheerleader costume I wore on Halloween.

"No, she didn't." I narrow my eyes. "But I have a question for you."

"What?" she snaps.

"More of a statement, really." I move closer to her, standing right in front of her. "I know you're fucking my husband."

Tabitha's face floods with expression. Shock. Fear. Anger. Finally, agitation, her eyes sharp, meeting my gaze.

"He was always mine," she hisses. "You know that."

I pick up the beautifully decorated chocolate raspberry cupcake sitting on a plate, with my name on a cream-colored name card by it. She used name cards for a party of three! How dumb does she think we are?

"Do you want me to eat this cupcake, Tabitha?" I yell at her. "Do you?"

I smash the cupcake into her face. Chocolate frosting sticks to her forehead. Fresh raspberry filling drips down her face.

I see something for the first time in my life.

Tabitha.

Speechless.

One Week Earlier

The hostess seats us at a table in the back of the café. The space is warm and homey, aromas of coffee and fresh-baked pie in the air. A brightly lit Christmas tree sits in the corner and lighted garlands are decked throughout the café.

"Two lattes, please," Anne orders when the server arrives. She looks at me, pausing, seeming a bit hesitant. "And two slices of key lime pie."

I nod. "Sure."

Anne takes a deep breath and sits back in her seat, nervously fiddling with her napkin, then looks at me. "I'm so glad we could meet today. There's something I need to tell you."

"OK." I smile, curious about what she'll say.

"This will probably shock you, so be prepared."

"Okay," I say hesitantly.

"My name used to be Danielle. We knew each other as children," she says, her gaze intent on me.

Confusion floods me. Danielle.

"Uh... Danielle? The girl we adopted?"

She nods.

"What? But... you disappeared. Went missing. Everyone thought you ran away." How could Anne possibly be Danielle? None of this makes any sense. Confusion and uncertainty race through me. She can't be her. Danielle ran away. We all assumed she was dead, she never came back, but how would Anne know about Danielle?

"It's more complicated than that," she replies. She holds out her hand and flips it over. We both stare at the long scar on her palm, the same scar I noticed at the pizza shop months ago.

"Remember the time you, Tabitha and I were baking together, and Tabitha was slicing strawberries? When you went to the bathroom, she did this to me. She stuck the knife into my palm and sliced me open. Then she held a towel over it, squeezing it to hurt more, and told me baking was only for her and you, before she called your mom for help. Do you remember that?"

I nod. I remember coming out of the bathroom and Tabitha squeezing a towel over Danielle's hand, calling Mom for help. I always wondered if Tabitha did something. She never liked Danielle from the moment our parents adopted her. Neither did Zach.

I stare at her, really look at her. My friend from so long ago. "It's really you."

She nods. "It is really me. Unbelievable as it may seem."

I grasp her hand across the table and squeeze, old memories flooding my mind of our short time spent together. Powerful memories of friendship and joy. Love floods my heart as I stare at my old friend. "I missed you so much when you were gone. We had such a special bond. I loved spending time with you."

Anne nods. "We do have a special bond. We still do."

A few tears roll down my face. "I'm so glad you're here. Tell me what happened."

Anne sighs. "Tabitha and Zach. They are the reason I disappeared."

FORTY-ONE

TABITHA

Three Weeks Earlier

"I know what I saw," Zach insists. His dark eyes dart around my kitchen where we sit drinking wine. He had barged in my front door, in a flurry, mumbling about a picture of Anne he saw on the Internet.

Danielle.

Anne is Danielle.

Danielle is Anne.

Now her familiarity to me makes sense. But how is she still alive?

We thought she was dead.

"Do you think Talia knows?" I ask.

He nods. "I'm sure she's told her. They are very friendly. More than Talia admits."

"I agree." I round the kitchen table and sit on his lap, giving him a long, hard kiss. "Do you think she knows about us?"

Zach and I have been sleeping together for about a year. While we've always been close, the physical part of our relationship started shortly before last Christmas. I'd been confiding in Zach for months about Grant's infidelity, then he walked over to my house with a box of Christmas ornaments Talia wanted to give me. Decorations I had made years ago, and she found at her house. Something was different that day: the way he stood too close to me, his familiar musky cologne encircling me, the closeness of our mouths and bodies. He kissed me once, gently, tentatively, testing me to see if I wanted him. And I did. I have always wanted him. And this time, I didn't think of what Talia wanted, only what I wanted. So the relationship with Zach was established before Anne arrived in Little Beak and, to be truthful, I never really suspected her of anything, at least at first. Grant's little story about problems at work was obviously an attempt to steer questions away from his numerous hotel charges and to squash any questions from me. All this drama was good though, for keeping Talia distracted from what was happening. Sure, I was upset by Grant's cheating, but I was used to it. The new love in my life was a different piece of the puzzle this time. Grant had cheated on me throughout our marriage, and I always felt isolated and alone. I never shared any of this with Talia; it was embarrassing. Now, I had Zach. I wasn't letting him go.

Sex with Zach is the best in my life; we connect on a deeply emotional level, plus he has certain attributes I'm surprised Talia didn't tell me about, but I was happy to discover on my own.

I love him and, more important, he loves me. He always has since we were kids. I know it. Talia knows it. My feelings run deep for him, but I knew Talia wanted him, so I stepped aside. I knew I could have Zach any time I wanted, but I chose to give him to Talia. She loved him. There was a time that I would do anything for Talia.

And I did.

With Zach's help.

But that Christmas last year I was sick of Grant's philandering. Kim was only one of many women he was screwing, his latest. His list of conquests dated back many years, and I was at a crossroads. Put up with it or get divorced. And divorce wasn't an option. I didn't want to give up my lifestyle and I didn't want to put up with it. I confided in Zach, and he became my safe haven. A shoulder to cry on. A love that I could always count on to be there for me.

At first it was only friendship; I knew I could trust Zach. I knew because of the secret we already shared for many years. Then when it turned physical, there was no going back to friendship after that. I struggled with what I was doing to Talia. I'm sleeping with my sister's husband. But I feel justified in doing it. Zach has always been mine; I just wasn't ready for him before. Now I am, I need to be with him. It's the right time for us.

He didn't want to be with Talia anymore. He loves her, in a way, but he loves me more. He told me he had been fantasizing about being with me for years. And now that he has me, he won't give me up. We talked about divorcing our spouses, but Grant's latest cheating escapade made me certain I would never divorce him. He was going to pay for what he'd been doing to me for years. And he paid with his life.

Zach came up with the idea of the hit and run. He stole a car, dressed completely in black, and I told him exactly when Grant would be going to the doughnut shop that morning. Because of him I got everything: the house, money, and the respect of a grieving widow. Zach gave me everything.

But now I owe him. I don't want to hurt Talia. I can't hurt Talia. Zach wants me to take care of her, like he took care of Grant for me. Why can't he divorce her? I have plenty of money. We can be together and be happy.

Zach refuses.

He wants her gone. No loose ends, just like I requested so many years ago. He says I owe him, and he is right.

No loose ends.

FORTY-TWO

ANNE

Halloween 2006

"Danielle, look at me!" Talia says, bursting into my bedroom. She dances around the room in a bright flowered dress, with matching headband, and brown tasseled boots we found at the thrift store last week. "I'm a hippie chick!"

"You look great!" I exclaim. "What about me?" I smooth the red and white pleats on the skirt of my cheerleader costume, one Talia wore last year. I turn my head to look in the mirror, tying my hair back with a bright red ribbon.

"I love it. That's one of my favorite costumes that Mom made for me," she replies, her hazel eyes bright with excitement. "It looks so good on you!"

We just ate breakfast and won't be going trick or treating until the evening, but we can't wait to put on our costumes. So, we do.

"Wait until you see Tabitha," Talia says. "She's so scary."

No different than any other day. As a fifteen-year-old girl, Tabitha is scarier to me than any monster under my bed.

And Zach.

When I moved here, almost a year ago, I was so happy to have a home. Nobody expects your mother to die when you're thirteen years old, and I never knew my father. Mr. and Mrs. Blake were my foster parents before they officially adopted me. I feel lucky to be living in their cozy farmhouse in Watkins Glen. They are kind to me, and I especially enjoy spending time with Mrs. Blake, who showed me how to knit. I still mourn my mother's death and knitting is a relaxing activity for me while I think of her. I know it sounds like an old lady's hobby, but my mom always said I am wise beyond my years. A little adult. At only thirteen years old, I already felt ancient.

Talia and I became fast friends. Her twin, Tabitha, is another story. She hates me. Talia and I love making crafts together, painting, making bead bracelets, anything that involves creativity. She is the best.

While Tabitha doesn't interact with me much, she does watch my every move. When I joined them to bake cupcakes one day, she sliced my palm open, and told me baking was something only she and Talia did together. I never joined them again.

Tabitha is ferociously protective of Talia and her parents, overbearingly so; and Zach, their best friend from down the road, is obsessive about Tabitha. Zach tracks every move Tabitha makes and accommodates anything she wants or wants to do. If she asked him to jump off a bridge, I'm sure he'd do it. One plus, she has a habit of sneaking off with Zach without Talia. Talia will get so involved with her crafts she doesn't even notice, and those are the best times, being alone with Talia or Mrs. Blake. I try to stay away from Tabitha and Zach. Neither of them like me, and they scare me, especially Zach, who will do anything Tabitha asks of him. He follows her around like a dog everywhere she goes.

"Let's get Mom's makeup; she has more than we do. We can put her darker blush and lipstick on you." Talia's voice breaks into my thoughts. "Ooh... I can put peace signs on my cheeks with mascara!"

"Yeah, let's do it," I agree, locking arms with my friend. We walk down the hall in search of makeup.

By afternoon, Talia is in bed with a stomach virus. She won't be going trick or treating. Mrs. Blake calls Zach's mother, to see if she could accompany us on the trick or treat route. She agrees.

Worry fills me at the thought of going with them, even with his mother along. I try to beg off, even saying I am sick, but Mrs. Blake doesn't buy it.

"I know you want to be a good friend to Talia since she's sick, but go out and have fun," Mrs. Blake says, smiling at me.

Now I trudge behind Tabitha, who wants to go to Zach's house early. She glances back at me, in full zombie makeup, and black clothing, then stops, waiting for me to catch up.

She grabs my hand and runs, dragging me with her. Instead of going to Zach's house, just a five-minute walk down a country road, she darts the other way, over the grassy hill toward the lake where we often eat picnic lunches.

"Why are we going down here?" I ask, trying to pull away. Panic swells through me. She has me in a deadlock.

"I want to show you something," she says breezily. She pulls so hard, I think my arm will break if I don't follow her. So, I do.

Sunset descends over the lake. Rich red and gold trees shimmering in the pleasant autumn evening. If I were here under different circumstances, I'm sure I'd enjoy the beauty. Today terror fills me.

Zach steps out from behind a tree. He too is dressed as a zombie. How original. He stares at me, incredibly disturbing in his scary face makeup.

I pull my arm hard, away from Tabitha, finally releasing it. Zach is by my side in a flash, grabbing me.

"Where are you going?" he asks in a menacing voice. White makeup on his face and black makeup around his eyes are perfect for his already ghoulish personality.

Tabitha grabs me again. "Why are you wearing my sister's costume?"

"What? Your mom gave me this to wear."

"Talia wore this costume last year. Talia is *my* sister! Not yours!"

Tabitha pushes me into the mud by the lake. I quickly get back up.

"I don't want you around her," Tabitha sneers at me. "Stay away from her and my mom."

"I live there," I say in a small voice. What am I supposed to do?

I see Zach out of the corner of my eye. Before I can move, he hits me in the head with a rock and I fall. I must have passed out for a few minutes. When I wake, they are talking about what to do with me.

"She's going to tell my parents," Tabitha says in a little girl voice. "What am I going to do?"

Zach clears his throat. The words he speaks sound much more like a man than a fifteen-year-old boy. "I'll take care of it."

In a swoop he picks me up. I struggle, clawing at his zombie face, kicking anything I can, but he's strong. Zach carries me to the lake. Fear spreads throughout me. He will kill me; I'm sure of it.

"Don't! I won't tell anyone!" I scream, my hair releasing from its ponytail, my bright red ribbon falling into the water. He pushes me down and holds me, his brown eyes now blackening, glazing over. I stare at him through the murky water and let go, sinking.

"No loose ends," is the last thing I hear him say before I sink into darkness.

· · ·

My eyes fly open, stinging from the water surrounding me. My head aches. I must have passed out for a few minutes. Was I dead during those minutes?

Terror floods me and adrenaline kicks in. I have to get out of here.

I will die soon if I don't.

The hazy water around me does little to guide me to safety. Panic pricks in every inch of my body. I have to move. Get out of here. I swim underwater as fast and as long as possible to what I hope is the back of the lake. I need air. If I remember correctly, there is a grove of tall grasses in the rear of the lake. I pray to come up inside of them.

Gasping as quietly as possible, my prayers are answered as I emerge in the middle of the weeds, mud and dead bugs squishing around me. I'm alive. My body spasming, my head throbbing from the gash on my forehead, I'm still alive.

How long was I knocked out?

It must not have been long. Voices from the other edge of the lake filter over to me. Tabitha talking about packing my suitcase and throwing it into the lake. She keeps repeating herself.

"They will think she ran away. They will think she ran away," she says repeatedly. Worry fills her voice She even cries, but Zach calms her with a soothing voice.

I tread water, eventually weaving myself through the weeds to the side of the lake along the bank, slopping in more mud, thicker here. The warm autumn afternoon breeze becomes stronger and colder as night moves in. Wet and cold, I shiver, but I will not step foot out of this water to risk running into either of them. I stay still, as still as possible, until I know it is safe to emerge. I wait until darkness fully descends. I hear Tabitha come down and drop something into the water, likely my suitcase, mumbling to herself. If people think I have run away, maybe that's a good thing. Nobody will look for me and drag me back to the Blake house. Once the suitcase is disposed of into the water, I'm certain they will go trick or treating with Zach's mother now. And I will get out of here.

I trudge out of the water, plodding along with each step. As night descends, the temperature drops and cold settles into my bones. I'd give anything for a warm coat or blanket, a cup of hot chocolate or steaming bowl of soup, to stave off the icicles forming in my body that become frostier with every single step I take. I'm freezing. My once pretty costume, torn and stained, hangs on me, the wetness only adding to my freezing body. Late October can be tricky like that, warm beautiful afternoon trans-forming into a cold, windy night, especially when you have spent hours soaking in a murky lake. I walk and walk. I am along the road now, at the side, easily able to hide if needed. I walk the opposite way Tabitha and Zach would travel. I walk on the road out of town.

The lonely road does little to calm my nerves, only more darkness looming ahead of me. I am completely on my own now. What am I going to do? Where will I go? I certainly can't go back to the Blake house. Even if I went back and told Mr. and Mrs. Blake about everything that had happened, I don't know if they would believe me: Tabitha is their daughter. And if by some miracle they did believe me, I still wouldn't be safe from her and Zach. They will find a way to get back at me, of that I'm certain. I need help. Nobody wants me and I'm not safe; I know what a dangerous situation I am facing alone. I am a thirteen-year-old girl completely on my own. I will not go back to foster care. I will survive on bugs and sleep in a ditch before that happens. I say another prayer and continue my journey, cold, wet, and alone.

A short time later, an old blue pickup truck drives past me. Should I try to stop it? I don't know. How else will I get out of here?

The truck stops. Then backs up.

Fear trickles through me. This stranger might hurt me too, but what other choice do I have?

"Do you need help?" the driver asks. He is a middle-aged man with a craggy face and kind eyes.

I nod and open the truck door, the smell of cinnamon gum casting a pleasant scent.

"I'm Charles Graveley," the man says, smiling warmly at me.

FORTY-THREE

TABITHA

Zach is the first to realize Anne's real identity. He is angry at Talia for turning her back on me and ignoring what I need from my sister, her time spent with Anne a particular irritation to him. After seeing the author photograph on Talia's laptop, he knew it was her. One picture revealing her true self.

Pale blue eyes.

She is smart wearing green contacts. The moment he saw that picture he knew she was Danielle, the foster kid we thought we murdered by the lake. He said he'd never forget her pale blue eyes staring up at him through the murky water. She haunts his dreams, but he'd do it again.

For me.

He'll do anything for me.

Danielle, who now goes by Anne, isn't dead. How she survived is unknown to us. After that Halloween night everyone thought she ran away; Zach and I left the lake after we were certain she sank to the bottom. I snuck into our house, threw some of her stuff in a suitcase, went back to the lake and threw it in. If a suitcase and her stuff was gone, she had to be a runaway, right?

Then I went over to Zach's and his mom took us trick or treating. I told her Danielle decided she didn't want to go. When I got home, I told my parents she decided not to go, and when they couldn't find her, they called the police. There were searches and Zach and I thought they would find her in the lake, but nothing. I told my mom that her suitcase and clothes were gone, so the police assumed she ran away, just as we had hoped. We joined the search ourselves, pretending we grieved her loss and hoped to find her alive. No leads and the search efforts ended after a few weeks. As if she simply vanished, which was fine with me. I didn't need her trying to take over my life. I was glad she was gone.

Now she's back, and Talia is her best friend again. Why my sister keeps choosing her over me will never make any sense to me. I'm sure Anne has spilled the beans about what happened at the lake all those years ago. Talia was probably even in on putting that stupid costume there to scare me. Talia has chosen whose side she wants to be on and now she will pay the consequences. Now she follows Anne around like she used to follow me. Anne purposefully left that creepy cheerleader costume on her bed for me to find. A direct message to me that she has come back for revenge; but why now? I have wondered so many times. Funny how something as simple as eye color can make you realize something that has been staring at your face for months. Her only tell is that weird way she cocks her head to the left when she looks at you. Nothing else about her reminds me of Danielle. My hesitation about Talia dissipates and I realize Zach is right. Once we know about Anne and observe her closeness with Talia, Zach and I know what needs to be done.

Kill them both.

FORTY-FOUR

TALIA

When Anne, whom I used to know as Danielle, told me everything last week, I was shocked. The story she told me was outlandish, but I believed her. The scar on her hand confirms she is Danielle. I don't know why Tabitha and Zach would have done what they did, and I certainly don't think they will hurt me, but Anne does. It is so crazy, but Anne has nothing to gain from the story. She is trying to help me. I remember the short, but close, friendship we had as children and then she was gone.

Missing.

Runaway.

Nobody knew for sure.

Time passed and she faded in my mind, in everyone's mind except my mother's. She always held a hope that she would hear from her again. She felt guilty that perhaps she hadn't made her comfortable enough in our house and that was why she ran away. I knew that wasn't true but wondered what had happened to her. I felt so bad for her knowing that she lost her mother. At thirteen years old, I couldn't imagine how I would handle such a loss and then go to live with strangers. She is braver than anyone else I know.

I know Tabitha hated her and was mean to her. Zach was cold with her too, but I never imagined either of them would be capable of what they did to her. My marriage to Zach has been rocky for the last year or so, probably even longer but I chose to ignore it. He always had his ups and downs, although the intensity of his outbursts toward me have increased. Now I know why. Although never directed at me, I recognize the darkness that lurks inside Tabitha and Zach. I've lived with each of them, know how manipulative each of them can be, but could I imagine them turning those claws of manipulation into me? Never. I love both and I thought each of them loved me, too.

I hold reservations about what brought Anne back to me. Her story seems fantastical, but some things in life are unexplainable. When she tells me about all she experienced, I take her words seriously.

The revelation cast everything over the last year into a new light. And especially Grant's death. Could that have been Tabitha's and Zach's doing? And if so, could I be next? If he had never had the affair with Kim, would life have continued? Zach and Tabitha conducting their relationship on the sly, me oblivious to anything, probably having a baby, or trying to, with Zach. Thank goodness, we never went through with IVF. If Zach and I had a baby together, we'd be bound for life in that capacity. Now, I can be completely free of him. It makes me sick how they manipulate me and how naïve I am to their actions. I always give the benefit of the doubt. I knew there was some darkness that lived in each of them, but I chose to ignore it and focus on the positive, the wonderful parts I love about each of them. And for that, I am punished.

My friendship with Anne ignites again as we spend more time together. I enjoy spending time with her, I always have: In a way she is the sister I really want. She doesn't criticize me, belittle me, or try to kill me, you know, the basics. We simply have fun together and respect each other.

I am Anne's friend.

FORTY-FIVE

ANNE

I tell Charles Graveley my entire story that night, from my mother dying of cancer, to the Blakes, to what happened at the lake. Everything spills out of me, including a flood of tears.

He nods but doesn't say much. He listens to everything I tell him and hands me a box of tissues sitting on the seat of his truck. He says his wife always makes sure the box is there; she says you never know when you need a tissue.

He takes me home that night to a small, cozy house in Ithaca he shares with his wife, Millie, and their sweet Yorkie, Bea. They become my family. Charles and Millie are an older couple, in their mid-fifties, and had always wanted children but were unable to have them. Adoption is out of the question; Charles has a criminal record for assault from years ago due to a bar fight before he met Millie and settled down. Millie home-schools me and we live a happy life, just the three of us, and little Bea. My prayer has been answered.

Eventually I change my name from Danielle to Anne, my middle name. Anne Graveley.

. . .

After my near-death experience, something unusual begins happening to me. An unexplained phenomenon.

Premonitions.

At first, the visions scare me. Premonitions don't allude to anything good coming up in your life or others'. They don't tell you who you will marry, or that you will be a successful author one day, or if you will win the lottery. No, they show danger in your future, impending danger, even death; but they are useful when interpretation can sway the danger from the intended. Now, I feel the premonitions are a gift. Something so unusual and uniquely my own.

The first one came when I was fourteen, a little over a year since I'd been living with the Graveleys. In the premonition, I somehow knew it was a Tuesday morning and Millie, I didn't call her Mom yet, and I drove to the grocery store. It was a rainy day and a car swerved over to our side of the road, hitting us head on. I continued to see this scene in my mind repeatedly, more details emerging. It was confusing. I wasn't dreaming, I was awake, but the images in my mind were sharp and clear as reality. As I learned throughout the years, if a premonition persists and grows in vivid details the likelihood of it coming true is certain. The way I'd describe it is a movie running in my mind and with each time it is shown to me, more close-ups of the details emerge that I need to focus on. In the past, I've had a few weak visions that eventually go away, not sure the purpose of those, but the strong ones give me all the information I need to make an impact for the better for the individual involved in the scene.

One Tuesday, Millie needed milk, bread, and a few other items. She asked if I would like to go to the grocery store with her. I looked outside, rain coming down in sheets and running down our short driveway. I knew today was when the accident would occur. I told Millie about my premonitions. She was an incredibly open-minded person and she believed me. We stayed home and, later that day on the news, they reported a head-on collision on the road we would have been on at the time we would have been traveling on it. No survivors.

My premonitions are real. I had a few more in my teens, even more in my twenties; all came to fruition. Then two years ago, I saw Talia in them. I tried to ignore it. I didn't know where Talia had ended up, but as much as I would have loved to have seen her, I was sure her devil sister and her lapdog wouldn't be far behind. I certainly did not want to be anywhere near Tabitha or Zach, if he was still in their lives. Sometimes, not as much now, but when I was younger, my nightmares were filled with images of the two of them, dressed as zombies, tormenting me by the lake. I never wanted to see either of them again.

The visions persisted, though, until I couldn't ignore them. Constantly I am back at the lake seeing Talia, and sometimes myself, drowning on that fateful Halloween night, reminding me of what Tabitha and Zach are capable of doing. If they could do it to me, they could do it to Talia. They have an advantage with her: She trusts them. I don't have any other premonitions, only that recurring one, which has consumed my thoughts on a regular basis. My fiancé, Danny Levinston, aka Dan from the bookstore, recently retired early from the FBI and was more than willing to help me with this venture I knew I must tackle. I couldn't allow Talia to die.

Danny and I did some research. We found out Talia was married to Zach, living next door to Tabitha in Little Beak, NY, only a short train ride from the city. They weren't that far from me. Talia married to Zach, that fact was the clincher. My heart sank. I had to intervene. I wasn't sure if Tabitha would hurt Talia, but Zach would have no qualms about it, especially if it put him in good favor with Tabitha.

He will kill her.

I am certain of it.

About a year ago, Danny rented the space next to Little

Beak Sweets; putting in a bookstore seemed like an obvious choice, especially for us since we met at one of my book signings four years ago. The main reason was to keep close tabs on the trio, but the bookstore has proved profitable, so that's a bonus.

Danny enjoys the quaint bookstore and the cozy town, even suggesting that we move here permanently after everything is settled with the twins.

I moved in next to Talia and Zach and things escalated quickly. Zach could sense I was a danger to him, but he wasn't sure why. He certainly did not appreciate my presence, nor did Tabitha. I made sure all the knives were put away when she was around.

The clarity of the premonition created such a vivid picture in my mind of Talia's impending death. I hadn't seen her in twenty years, but the twins looked much the same, just matured. Same long honey-golden hair, slim bodies and doe-like hazel eyes. Zach looks different. I wouldn't have known him, and he hadn't appeared in the vision. He's much better looking than when he was younger, but when he looks at Tabitha, he has the same infatuated stare as when he was fifteen years old. I often wonder how he kept those feelings under wraps while married to Talia. How did she not notice?

When I moved here, I worried they may recognize me, but after a thorough assessment I realized the only feature that may have given me away were my pale blue eyes, so contacts were needed. When they knew me, I had mid-length mousy brown hair, crooked teeth and a chubby body. Now my hair hangs long and curly, my body is trim and lithe, my teeth straight. I knew I'd pass their inspection.

Tabitha is playing the games she likes to play. Anything to keep her the center of attention. Sure, she didn't like me, she didn't like me spending time with Talia, but she is enjoying the drama. Sneaking around my house, getting Talia into a tizzy about me, making smart comments to me and about me. Fun for her. Then, there is a shift.

They know I am Danielle.

They know I sense their plans for Talia.

They know they are in trouble.

I wonder how the timeline would have played out if I never arrived in Little Beak. If I ignored the nagging premonitions and never came to this town. What would be the tipping point for Zach and Tabitha to take Talia out and dump her in that lonely lake? I guess I'll never know.

I'm here now.

Oh, the fun I had setting up the cheerleader costume in my bedroom for the sisters to find. My guess that they would break into my house again was spot on. So much fun. My unspoken message to Tabitha. I am here and she's in trouble, although I'm not sure if she knew I was Danielle, or only someone that knew what they did that day by the lake. Regardless, I enjoyed the cat and mouse game with her, and I'm sure that costume sent her reeling. Perhaps a bit strange to keep such a thing, maybe most people would have thrown out the costume since I was almost killed while wearing it, but to me it was a tangible reminder that I'm a survivor and that I can make it through anything life throws at me. When I wrote *The Secret* it was loosely based on my attempted murder at the lake. Writing that story proved cathartic for me, reliving the terror, but also the realization that I was still here, healthy, and alive, despite Zach's efforts to silence me. And if they had gotten away with murder on that Halloween night, Talia would be lying on the lake floor with cement blocks tied to her feet, I'm sure of it.

Danny set up a hidden camera in the bakery, approved by Talia. Footage from yesterday shows Tabitha baking some delicious chocolate raspberry cupcakes, the batter divided between two bowls, with an ingredient she adds to one bowl from a small vial retrieved from her purse—my guess, ground foxglove, a deadly poison. I'd noticed the flowers growing in Tabitha's garden when I took my lasagna after Grant's death.

Late last night camera footage was finally sent over from the Long Island Expressway. Two images of the stolen car and its driver. One image shows the driver yanking off his ski mask. Another image shows the driver stuffing the remainder of a giant cream doughnut into his mouth; the ski mask must have been in the way. Both images show the same man. He's been under surveillance since the evidence was received.

Zach.

FORTY-SIX

TALIA

Monday

Anne and I share a look. The time has come. A reckoning. The secrets swirling around Little Beak finally will be known to all. If someone would have told me my life as I know it will be altered in such a fleeting moment, I'd be shocked. A lovely Christmas tea suddenly takes on an entirely different tone, one I'd been expecting.

Police rush into the dining room, apprehending Tabitha so fast, she's still wiping the frosting off her face. Shock springs in her eyes as her rights are being read and her hands put into handcuffs. More commotion outside the dining room as officers bolt upstairs and soon came back down with a handcuffed Zach, the doughnut eater. I stare at him, my husband, my attempted murderer. He avoids my gaze and stares at the floor. Anne and I watch as everything unfolds in front of us. My mind goes back in time...

The summer after we all graduated from college changed my life. I was working at a bookstore; Zach started a new job at a bank in a town about twenty minutes from us, and Tabitha planned her wedding to Grant.

Something simmered between me and Zach that summer. We'd always had friendship, and I'd wanted more for years, but he had never seemed interested in exploring anything beyond friendship. Watching Tabitha pick out venues, dresses, and menus for all her wedding festivities made that longing inside for something with Zach even stronger.

Finally, he felt it too. He asked me out on a date, a real date, not just as friends. We went out to dinner and a movie. We held hands in the movie theater, and he kissed me goodnight at my front door later that evening. Everything I dreamed of for years. I loved him. I had for years. And I think everyone knew it.

I'm not completely naïve. I saw his furtive glances at Tabitha. I knew he harbored a crush on her for years, but we all have crushes here and there. I was certain his attention was now solidly on me and building a relationship together.

As things progressed, that's exactly what happened. We built our own life, not as glamorous as Tabitha and Grant, but that was okay, it was our life. The year or so we spent living upstate close to our parents, when Tabitha and Grant lived in Little Beak, was probably the best of my life. I wasn't living in her shadow. I wasn't second best. Just Talia. Talia and Zach. We were happy together.

Maybe we should have never moved to Little Beak, but it probably wouldn't have made a difference. Zach's love, or maybe a better word would be obsession, for Tabitha didn't die; it only remained dormant for a period. He couldn't compete with Grant, he knew, so he settled for second best: me, until he got another chance with Tabitha...

Now, I stare at him, standing there so pathetic, handcuffed, head down, and wonder what I ever saw in this shell of a man. What an actor he is, and I play along, believing I was someone special in his eyes, but no, I'm only a pawn.

I debate addressing him, screaming how much he hurt me, but decide against it. He isn't worth it. I have nothing to say to him. I will never talk to that monster again. He is dead to me.

"What are you doing in my house?" Tabitha yells. "I'm calling my lawyer."

An officer comes in and places all the baked goods into evidence bags to be processed by the lab later. He even takes the red teapot with small painted candy canes and the candies on the white three-tiered display. Every food item bagged and labeled, including the smashed cupcake lying on the floor and the frosting he wiped from Tabitha's face, quickly depositing it into an evidence bag.

I stare at Tabitha. She has a good side, although she hides it well. As much as I'm shocked by Zach's actions, I'm appalled by her more. I truly never thought she would harm me. Others, yes, but not me. I always felt like she protected me in her own way, yet the one I need protection from is her.

In all the chaos around me, a memory keeps playing in my mind: me and Tabitha, in our parents' house, sprawled out in the large bed we shared in our room. We are around fourteen or so and Tabitha is painting my fingernails, a bright glittery pink, while my glittery pink toenails dry. She takes special care applying the polish, wiping any small stray smudge landing on my skin. Music plays in our shared room, and we laugh and talk while she finishes my nails. She is good at doing nails, but most of all I enjoy the closeness of her, without all her pretension. Just me and her being sisters.

Now that is over. Now I sit at a dining room table with a poisoned cupcake she served to me. Well, now the offending cupcake is in an evidence bag.

"What is going on?" Tabitha yells again. She turns, staring at Zach. "Why is Zach here?" she asks, in a calmer voice, playing surprised.

I move closer to her. "Stop lying, Tabitha! You know why

he's here," I yell, glaring at her. "And you know exactly what you were going to do to *me*." Fury burns inside me. I can't believe she would turn on me like this. She is my sister. My twin! She betrays me for Zach, why? "How could you do this to me?"

"I don't..." Tabitha's eyes widen, directing her gaze at Anne. Her eyes darken. Her voice growls. "You did this."

"You're damn right," replies Anne, her pale blue eyes bright and happy. "I did."

FORTY-SEVEN

TABITHA

Two Years Later

I add the sprinkles to Genna's birthday cake, double chocolate, and stare at my creation for a moment. Genna is celebrating her fiftieth birthday, the last ten years spent in prison, for murdering a school crossing guard. I'm glad I can still bake in prison; my skills make me quite popular with the inmates and prison staff. I'm known as The Baker in the maximum-security women's prison that Grant's family pushed for during sentencing, not a bad nickname, compared to others.

I can bake, work out, and have an ongoing fling with Remy, a darkly handsome night guard, which secures me some luxuries like silk pillowcases, high thread-count sheets and my favorite brand of moisturizer. I am making the most of my situation. I take charge, like always, and figure out a way to make things work for me in here.

I think of the life I had in Little Beak with Grant, Cole, Talia and Zach. It didn't seem real, almost as if it were a dream. What a beautiful life it was. I wish I would have appreciated it more while I lived it. Why did I make the decisions I made? I don't have any answers, other than greed and jealousy. It cost me everything. I'll never get to see my sweet Cole grow up.

Zach is persuasive: If it wasn't for him, I would never have agreed to hurt Talia. He was so insistent on it, as if somehow if I did that, my love for him was true. Ridiculous, I know, but I realize now I can only blame myself for my own actions. I also realize Zach is poison, no pun intended, to me and Talia. Would our lives have been different if he was never in it? Who knows?

I miss Talia. I miss spending time with her. I miss everything about her. She will always be my best friend. I doubt I'll ever see her again and I can't blame her. She'll always be a part of me.

She's my twin.

FORTY-EIGHT

TALIA

Two Years Later

I put another batch of vanilla latte cupcakes into the oven and set the timer. The door jingles and I walk out to the front counter. Claire left for the day, so it is just me. I put six cupcakes into a pink box and wish the customer a good day.

Today is a good day. My divorce from Zach is final today. Six months ago, Tabitha signed over her part of the business to me. I guess she views it as a peace offering or maybe she is just giving up. Grant's parents make it their mission to keep her, and Zach, locked up in prison and they have the expensive lawyers to do it. Either way, I don't care. I'm now the sole owner of Little Beak Sweets and I am single. At least I'm moving forward.

Zach and Tabitha both sent me numerous letters, many more from Tabitha than Zach, but I open none of them. I throw them into an oak blanket chest that sits at the foot of my bed. I may read them one day, or I may not. I doubt I'm missing much. When I think of their scheme to get rid of me and Anne, I feel sick. This was my family. How they could imagine doing something like this to me is beyond my understanding.

Digitalis, derived from Tabitha's foxgloves, was found in the cupcakes for Anne and me, also in the teapot. There was also a rented SUV in Tabitha's garage along with two cement blocks. While they did not admit it, the plan was to wait until the poison killed us, load us into the SUV and dump our bodies into the same lake where they thought they murdered Anne that day so many years ago. The GPS on Tabitha's vehicle showed they were recently at the location of the lake.

Our house was sold in the divorce agreement. I live in the apartment over the bakery for now. We had previously used it for storage, but it is a comfortable home for me, at least temporarily. It feels good to clean it out, paint the walls, buy new furniture, a fresh start for me. It's small, but all I need. I'm not sure what my next step will be in life, and I am not in a rush. I have a new roommate, a furry one named Sprinkles, the sweetest Goldendoodle puppy you'll ever meet.

Cole lives with his grandparents in Manhattan. He visits me once a month here and I visit him a couple times in the city every month. He also stays with my parents for a weekend once a month. He is doing well as expected given the circumstances. He is always happy to see me but struggling with the loss of his parents. Tabitha writes him letters, which are monitored by Grant's parents. I imagine he will be a grown man before Tabitha sees him again, if ever.

Anne and Danny got married last year. They bought an older Victorian house at the end of Main Street in Little Beak and are refurbishing it. Anne's trilogy, *Premonition*, was a huge hit and was recently optioned for a Netflix series. Danny kept the bookstore; he enjoys it so much. My parents are devastated by Tabitha's and Zach's actions. They visit Tabitha from time to time, more infrequent lately. They can't understand, nor I, how she made the decisions that she did, and visiting takes a toll on them, so they have decided to take a break from seeing her. They focus on Cole, and my relationship with them is as close as ever. One bright spot: They were able to reconnect with Anne, who they knew as Danielle, and this is incredibly meaningful to my mother, who blamed herself for her disappearance. She is able to let go of that guilt, at least.

I glance at the cupcake clock hanging over the counter. Half an hour until I close the bakery and go upstairs to my apartment to get ready for my date tonight. Danny set me up with his friend, Special Agent Mike Ford. A finalized divorce and a first date on the same day. Who knows what my future holds?

Despite it all, I miss Tabitha. The Tabitha I thought I knew. I always thought she would be there for me, no matter what, and I never could have imagined she would want to hurt me, erase me from her life. I struggle to accept this fact. I don't know if I will ever fully accept it.

Lately, an old memory has been circulating in my mind: It is from when Tabitha and I were about nine years old. We take a walk on a cool fall day, through the woods and up to our favorite meadow located at the top of a tall hill overlooking the valley. Wildflowers stand tall in the still green grasses, blowing, and waving in the slight breeze. This place always seems magical to me, a place we visited many times, kind of like our own secret garden. We put flowers in our hair, roll around in the smooth grass, until we get itchy, then smooth out our long hair, removing pieces of grass and flowers, plucking another fresh bloom to wear.

Mom packs us each a bagged lunch—peanut butter and jelly for me, my favorite; ham and cheese, Tabitha's favorite—so we find the spot with the best view and pull out our sandwiches. She has hers out first and scowls.

"Ham and cheese again?" she mutters.

"That's your favorite," I say.

"It's not what I want today," she says, smiling. "Give me yours."

I hesitate. I don't want to. I don't particularly like ham and cheese, certainly not more than peanut butter and grape jelly, but I hand over my sandwich.

Tabitha's smile widens. "Exactly what I want. You're a good sister."

She's right. I am the good sister. She always gets exactly what she wants with no regards to my needs. I won't say I was unaware of this in the past—I know who she is—but never thought she would go to this extent.

And Zach. I wasn't as surprised by him. He's always been volatile and unstable as long as I have known him, but when things were good, they were so good that I overlooked the rest. I guess when you love someone, even know something is wrong within them, you just keep going, enjoying the good times and ignoring the bad. He was my first, but he won't be my last. I know if I do find love again, it won't be with someone I have to constantly maintain, but an equal, loving relationship for both of us. I hope to never see Zach again.

Will I see Tabitha again?

I don't know. I want to say no but can't say it for sure. She is a part of me.

She's my twin.

A LETTER FROM THE AUTHOR

Huge thanks for reading *The Secrets Next Door*; I hope you were hooked as the dynamic between Talia and Tabitha played out. If you want to join other readers in hearing all about my new releases and bonus content, you can sign up for my newsletter!

www.stormpublishing.co/sally-royer-derr

If you enjoyed this book and could spare a few moments to leave a review that would be hugely appreciated. Even a short review can make all the difference in encouraging a reader to discover my books for the first time. Thank you so much!

The Secrets Next Door developed from creative brainstorming between my editor, Emily Gowers, and myself. As I formed the outline, it was exciting to see the distinctive personalities of the twin sisters, Talia and Tabitha, take shape. Each has a unique voice and reasons for their actions. I had so much fun writing about them, and I hope you had fun reading their story.

Thanks again for being part of this amazing journey with me and I hope you'll stay in touch—I have so many more stories and ideas to entertain you with!

Sally

KEEP IN TOUCH WITH THE AUTHOR

www.sallyroyer-derr.com

facebook.com/SallyRoyerDerrAuthorPage

x.com/sallyroyerderr

instagram.com/srderr

bookbub.com/profile/sally-royer-derr

tiktok.com/@sallyroyerderr

ACKNOWLEDGEMENTS

First and foremost, I want to thank my editor, the insightful and delightful Emily Gowers. Your excitement for my writing, excellent editorial direction and creative collaboration have made creating this book an amazing process. I enjoy working with you so very much!

Thank you, Oliver Rhodes, and the entire team at Storm Publishing, for giving me a chance to present my writing to your audience. I am so grateful for this opportunity.

Thank you, Mike, for your constant love and support of me and my writing career. Also, for all the laughter and inside jokes we share. Thank you to my wonderful family and friends who get as excited as I do when talking about my book updates.

Huge thanks to my incredibly supportive readers—you are the best!

Made in United States
Orlando, FL
13 March 2024

44734127R00148